# The Chemical Factor

## A. G. Hayes

I0662928

Savant Books and Publications
Honolulu, HI, USA
2015

Published in the USA by Savant Books and Publications
2630 Kapiolani Blvd #1601
Honolulu, HI 96826
http://www.savantbooksandpublications.com

Printed in the USA

Edited by Kaethe Kauffman
Cover design by Daniel S. Janik
Cover images: "Cunard R. M. S. 'Queen Mary' Postcard" from
Photoree/Marxchivist - used under creative commons 2.0 "public
domain" license, and Couple Woman Man Detective Secret Agent
Criminal Silhouette Photo © Pixattitude | Dreamstime.com

13-digit ISBN: 9780996325547

# Dedication

To my wife Connie who sailed aboard the Queen Mary from Southampton to New York in 1948; we were married in Los Angles, in December.

# Chapter 1

Angina pectoris. Dr. Gordon Metcalf ground the heel of his right hand into his chest. He was a chemist, not a medical doctor. For weeks he ignored the shortness of breath, the slight pauses in heartbeat. But this...he was dizzy, on the verge of losing consciousness when the chamber in his heart finally pulsed.

He waited. The spindly fingers of his left hand gripped the rail of the outdoor veranda that ran the length of his home. He sucked up air until his reed-thin body, down to less than a hundred pounds now, straightened, then sagged with deflation.

It was eleven-thirty when the news flashed across the television screen. He quickly calculated the time: eight-thirty in California, three hours behind Panama. Metcalf's heart had literally paused when he learned that the *Queen Mary* was in danger of being destroyed.

*Dear God! What have I done? I never thought...*

It hadn't occurred to him that the ship, so big and so seemingly indestructible, might one day be in jeopardy. What could he do? An old man, weak, maybe even at the end. There was only one thing to do.

He took a piece of paper he had kept in a drawer and dialed the 202 area code number written there, breaking his fourty-seven-year silence.

A live woman, not a menu of choices, responded: "FBI headquarters."

"I need to speak to an agent. Hurry, please."

The Bureau believed him to be dead. Of course, he'd planned it that way in 1967. It bought him these peaceful, nearly guilt-free years on Contadora. But now, there was so much he felt he had tell the Bureau and so little time left. How can a breathless old man compress so many years of distorted reasoning on his part into a few minutes of telephone conversation?

After being transferred from extension to extension, he was connected to an agent.

"I can't go into my rationale at this time," he said, "but when I disappeared in 1967, I took with me a briefcase containing the results of a scientific experiment I had been working on at Neogenetic Conveyance Industries in Middlesex, UK division. I boarded the *Queen Mary* on her final voyage to Long Beach, California. I didn't think anyone knew I was on board."

"Obviously, no one did, sir," the agent said crisply. "You eluded the FBI, the National Security Agency, CIA and British Intelligence. We, in fact, instigated a futile worldwide search."

"Then you're familiar with the experiment?"

"Familiar with its existence, not particulars, sir."

It was obvious to Metcalf that he was talking to a veteran. But the man sounded nervous, eager, and probably unable to believe what he was hearing. After all this time, years after the trail went cold and his predecessors deemed the file inactive, here was the principal player, calling to say he was alive.

"You were quite clever, Dr. Metcalf," the man added.

When Metcalf made the decision to board the ship, he knew that, despite his attachment to the scientific community, he was the type of person who could easily fall through the cracks of civilization and be lost to the world.

"Not clever enough," Metcalf wheezed. "Someone, a Latin unknown to me, followed me on board the ship. He attacked me one night," he paused, hearing his breath sound like dry whistles. "I fought him off and I…I believe that I disfigured him for life. I couldn't let him get hold of the briefcase, you understand."

"Yes, sir. I know."

"Before I left the lab in England, I placed the compound in a specially constructed container."

He stopped abruptly, his feelings about the receptacle stung his mind. Secretly, he had dubbed it The Devil's Crucible, because he considered the contraption as a vessel whose depths seethed and boiled with a flesh-eating mixture that would grind through bone as surely as a chain saw. It was conceived by a part of his brain that must have been under the spell of Satan himself.

"Well," he said, once he was able to go on, "I put the compound in its container that, in turn, went into a briefcase reinforced with steel, and I took it onto the ship." He stopped again, a series of raspy coughs eating up ten seconds on the line.

"For reasons I don't have time to explain now, I'd intended to hurl it overboard. But I underwent a change of heart and decided to relinquish it to the United States' authorities in Long Beach at the end of the voyage."

Another pause and more gasps followed by a deep, punctuating sigh.

"Of course, once I knew the Latin was after it, I had to hide it. Somewhere where it could not be found, and would remain safe until I summoned the courage to notify the authorities. I had no *choice* but to hide it. Don't you see?"

The agent seemed to be holding his breath. "Hide it, sir?"

Metcalf heard the horror of his own words. Sweat moistened his face and he swiped a hand across his wet upper lip. "Yes, I hid it, then jumped ship in Panama. I've been living here on the small island of Contadora off the southeast coast of Panama ever since."

"Then, the briefcase containing this compound is…"

"Yes. On the *Queen Mary*, in Long Beach, California. God forgive me."

Sickeningly, he sensed the agent's mind ticking off some of the deadly combinations of volatile chemicals that must be in the briefcase. The chemicals themselves were harmless, inert, so long as they remained undisturbed and were not exposed to extreme temperature.

Metcalf's voice was a soft rattle now. "I imagine that you heard the news about the *Queen Mary* on television."

There was stunned silence on the other end of the line. Metcalf knew that he did not need to tell the agent about the madman on the ship and the firebombs he planned to detonate.

The bombs would burn the tinder-dry decks at a temperature as high as four thousand degrees Fahrenheit. Steel melted at three thousand degrees.

"Are you at home, sir?" the agent finally asked.

"Yes, but let me tell you exactly where on the ship the briefcase is hidden."

"No!" the agent stopped him, "Not on the phone. Look, Doctor, please, just tell me where you are. Give me your address and don't call or talk to anyone. We have people at the Consular Section of the U.S. Embassy on Panama Bay in Panama City. They'll fly out to the island and should be there within the hour."

But, if he had to wait for the agents from Panama City to arrive, he was afraid either he wouldn't last or, worse, the Latin might beat them. Somehow, now that he'd broken silence, the Latin would know and find him.

"Hurry," Metcalf wheezed.

# Chapter 2

"Click." The sound of a tape recorder being turned off.

"That concludes a phone call that's thirty-five years too late." Agent Falk muttered to himself. "We've all been living on borrowed time." Pushing back his chair he stretched his six-foot frame admonishing himself, "Get to work."

The recording had been sent to Cerberus HQ and had been forwarded to him; that action itself indicated the urgency of the call. The FBI was not in the habit of passing anything to anyone. Glancing at his watch, Falk knew there was still one very important factor missing: Agent Susan Koski, his partner in the everlasting battle against international corruption and the destruction of the United States. There was no time to waste.

# Chapter 3

"Wait, Frank, hold on a second," Joseph Falk said. He was on the phone in his parents' home in Studio City, California, and the caller, his Washington Bureau Chief, was new on the job and fair game for second-guessing. "How can we be certain this guy has in fact planted bombs on the Queen Mary?" Falk didn't want it to be true. "It could be a hoax. After 9/11, everybody's ready to believe anything."

Frank Heeley was breathless with excitement. "No way, Falk, no hoax. The guy left a note in his apartment flatly stating his plans. And the local authorities found evidence of explosives there. And he was sighted on board earlier by one of the ship's personnel. This guy, Jack Bonecutter's his name, was a reluctant but expert demolition man when it came to personnel mines and explosives in Nam, and is now a Hollywood screenwriter. He's also a certified schizophrenic who has obviously gone over the edge."

"But why does he want to destroy this ship?"

Heeley sighed. "That, I don't know. Look, my information from Long Beach PD is sketchy, but it seems that today is the anniversary of the ship's maiden voyage, back in 1936.

Bonecutter has been obsessed with her since he was a boy. He has something like eighty websites bookmarked on his computer describing every detail about her, from her tonnage to how many freakin' rivets it took to put her together.

"His note said that he resents her being permanently docked in the Port of Long Beach and 'prostituted,' transformed, I suppose, from what he saw as a majestic, seagoing castle into a floating tourist trap, hotel and shopping mall. He says he wants to 'set her free', so to speak."

Falk knew the situation was serious, but he had arrived in California only last night. "I don't know, Frank."

"Look, Joe," Heeley interrupted, "we're talking about a mammoth ocean liner, the Queen Mary. The ship weighs almost eighty thousand tons, and is over a thousand feet long, one hundred feet longer than the Titanic and twelve decks high. It's permanently docked in one of the busiest ports in the United States. Cruise ships leave there every day for Mexico, Alaska, you name it, destinations all over the world." Heeley talked fast, hurrying to get the facts out.

"Our alleged bomber is hidden on board and plans to blow himself up with the ship. He's planted ten homemade incendiary devices at various locations only he knows, to be ignited at eight o'clock tonight by a remote-controlled detonator he has on his person."

Healey paused. Falk offered no response. "It's a nightmare," Healey continued. "I just spoke to LBPD, and they're already evacuating the ship, but there's one thing they don't know."

"Frank, it's only nine a.m. local," Falk broke in. "Negotiators have eleven hours to locate, engage and subdue this individual."

"We *could* detail a team on this end or scramble one from the local field office, but that would take more time than we want to spend. Moreover, we want our involvement to be as minimal as possible; one or two people, tops," said Heeley, continuing, "Joe, you're one of the best agents the Bureau's got. And you're less than fifteen minutes away by military chopper, which, by the way, is on standby at Van Nuys airport." Heeley took a deep breath. "We need to get someone on that ship immediately."

"On the ship. You can't communicate with this guy from dockside? You want me to board a vessel that you're telling me is about to be blown up?"

Heeley may have been new to his position, promoted when Falk's previous chief was murdered during a Bureau investigation, but he was quick with the standard vernacular. "Did anyone ever tell you, Agent Falk, that working for the Federal Bureau of Investigation was a picnic?"

"Hey, Frank, I'm with Rover Division. My job is to sniff out terrorists, thugs, rogue militia groups and the like. This is not my station. For this assignment you need a good man from a First Response unit with…"

"We need *you*, Joe. When you and agent Koski literally saved this country's ass by uncovering those responsible for the serial killing of all those lawyers in Nevada, you merited the commendations you received."

Falk groaned.

Heeley's voice saying, "Hey, come on, Joe," recalled Falk to the present emergency. "Frank, why us? Can't the local authorities handle this?"

"Because there's more to this situation than we can risk with the locals. My orders were to assign you."

Heeley's tone had risen a few decibels, and Falk heard him clear his throat to bring it back under control. He knew the last remark was no argument. Heeley held the title, but they both knew who the superior agent was.

Then he added, "And because we are already involved."

Falk leaned toward the kitchen table and set down the mug of coffee he'd been holding in his left hand. "To what extent?"

Heeley sighed. "Eighty years ago our government bungled a top-secret assignment connected with the Queen Mary. The assignment involved a scientist who was working in England and is now in Panama. British Intelligence has its panties in a bunch and is threatening to get involved directly this time if we can't resolve it."

"British Intelligence. Shit! This is going to be a fucking circus!"

Until last year Falk had always been a loner. He preferred to live the roaming life in the field as part of the FBI's elite Rover Division. There he was free to make his own decisions. He had proved himself to be dangerous by the long list of convictions he amassed.

But the Nevada assignment that paired him with Special Agent Susan Koski changed all that. He thought it was possible that his developing feelings for her made him a better man.

Professionally, however, Falk secretly felt diminished because he was forced to work with someone as a team, making him one-half of a successful effort, one-half of what he once was. And now he wished she were here. He sighed.

"Okay, tell me about this so-called bungled assignment and the scientist in Panama."

Heeley's voice dropped to a harsh whisper. "Are you alone?"

"Yes, I'm alone."

"And this is a secure line?"

"Damn it, Frank, you know it is!"

As Heeley explained, Falk knew that Jack Bonecutter was about to destroy more than himself and an old ship.

The Chemical Factor

# Chapter 4

Jack Bonecutter fell into a black abyss, his legs and arms flailing furiously, hands thrashing, grasping for something, anything, to stop his wild descent. He grabbed at the madness of empty air, twisting from side to side, clawing for rungs of the ladder he gambled was there. His temples throbbed, and the beat echoed in his ears, his arms, his chest.

One hand, then the other, finally caught a rung. His feet, too, found support against the blind darkness that sucked him downward. He clung to the ladder, gasping for breath, nerve endings prickling and adrenaline pumping. Gradually the thumping in his chest subsided, and he breathed normally again.

For only a moment he released one hand to wipe a dense gauze of cobweb from his face. He was right; the wooden ladder his grandfather helped build was still intact, after over seventy-five years.

In 1934, the ladder was bootlegged as a convenience for the original builders in Scotland. It was a means by which they could stay inside, protected from the raw winds of the Clyde as they moved from top deck to the bottom of the ship. Bonecutter was thankful for their ingenuity.

He was convinced that no one but himself remembered the shaft and the ladder, unless the grandchildren of others who worked beside his grandfather were aware, which seemed improbable.

Hits to the Queen Mary web pages were from the curious, not the well informed. Her seductive secrets were forgotten as surely as her freedom was abandoned to crass commercial captivity.

The bridge was the nerve center of every ship, where the helm and other navigational equipment were located. The chartroom was small and spare. It contained a long, low bench built into the wall, a floor heater, wall panels for voltmeters and control lights, stacked wall cabinets for maps, and a large oak chart table where navigational maps had been laid out when the ship was at sea. Beneath the table that was more than waist high and built to accommodate a standing man, was a cupboard three and a half feet high and three feet wide and deep.

When the Queen Mary was in service, this cupboard was used for miscellaneous directional materials, but it had stood empty for years, its wooden floor gathering dust. The cupboard floor contained a flat trapdoor, the access to the long, vertical ladder to which Bonecutter now clung. He originally planned to carefully explore the shaft and test the ladder. However, the earlier appearance of two evacuating personnel on the bridge obliged him to rip open the wooden door on the floor and drop, feet first, into the darkness.

Now he slid one leg from the wooden rung and rotated his foot, relaxing his leg muscles, then repeated this movement with his other leg. He planned to balance on the ladder for many hours.

Here, in this dark shaft, he must remain hidden until it was time to go back up to the chart room and depress the small red dot on the remote in his shirt pocket.

He was safe here. Security, in their evacuation efforts, had checked the chart room. They would check the bowels of the ship hundreds of feet below. Bonecutter was suspended between the two.

He saw nothing; the cool dank blackness of his surroundings clung to him like shrink-wrap. He was aware of a hollow roar, like the sound of the ocean one heard in a conch shell, but loud and piercing.

Above the roar he heard the wail of sirens. Good. That meant everything was proceeding according to plan. His agent, Pete Powers, had called the police after finding the note Bonecutter left in full view in his apartment. The evacuation had begun in earnest.

His design was for the police to have plenty of time to get everyone off the ship. He didn't want to harm anyone.

Oh God!

He suddenly remembered he'd forgotten to take down the printout he had tacked above the desk in his apartment. His scalp prickled. Printed from one of his websites, the paper displayed a cross-section of the ship, on which he circled in red marker the exact location he chose for each bomb.

*Damn! At least I remembered to delete the page from the hard drive, so the police won't find it when they confiscate the computer*, he thought. *Meant to bring the printout. Could be a costly mistake unless Pete Powers and the police miss it. Things in plain view are often overlooked. Who am I kidding?*

But there was no turning back. For one agonizing moment, he feared one of his spells was about to overtake him. His skull seemed to shrink, and pressure built in his temples, a sign that he needed the medication he had decided to discontinue weeks ago.

Sounds, not voices, not words, but discordant music as if from a warped dulcimer filled his head. He did what he usually did: He waited. He concentrated on the eternal peace he expected when this day and night were over. This time the spell did not materialize and the shrinking feeling passed.

He mentally retraced his steps. Had he forgotten anything else? Had he chosen the best possible locations for his bombs? It had taken him nearly an hour to hide them on board, just before he dove into this shaft.

He was proud of his bombs. He'd spent days constructing the nests of explosives. He was surprised at the ease with which he obtained the needed materials from Internet sources. These included the powerful transmitter that allowed him to trigger the bombs prematurely, should an unfortunate circumstance arise to make that necessary.

Each bomb resembled a meat pie approximately eight inches in diameter. The "meat" was a sticky mixture the grunts in Nam called "foo," because that was the sound it made when ignited. As he put the bombs into place, he inserted electronic fuse-receivers in each.

Now, with their deadly potential in check, the receivers

awaited his command. They would respond to a transmitted signal, spark each bomb's explosive, gelatinous core, and splatter liquefied fire in every direction. The firestorm created would burn with an intensity of four thousand degrees Fahrenheit. Because the wooden decks of the Queen Mary were more than seven decades old and combustive as kindling, they would quickly ignite and the result would be unstoppable.

A mental vision of a torrent of flame flashed across his mind like an inferno, caused a momentary sense of misgiving. He was about to take from the world what he considered to be the ultimate ocean liner: the quadruple somersault, the grand slam, the quad axel of ocean-going vessels. In the past she routinely crossed the North Atlantic, carrying nearly two thousand passengers in graceful, felicitous splendor.

The Queen Mary had rare, almost human character that Bonecutter felt certain would never again be captured in a vessel. Despite the fact that on her maiden voyage she crossed the Atlantic in four days, twenty-three hours fifty-six minutes, Bonecutter insisted that she was much more than eighty tons of massive power.

Her lavish interiors were superior to all. While built to endure, one had only to envision her spacious ballrooms and salons in different lights to concede she was, in fact, a palace. Marble columns, rich thick Brussel carpets, ornamental paintings and lustrous draperies left an air of magnificence.

By night, all windows were ablaze with light, her broad, long ballrooms brilliantly illuminated by enormous crystal chandeliers.

A sudden deep involuntary sigh jolted Bonecutter's chest. He let go the vision of her glory days. she, like so much Bonecutter prized, had been devalued.

The green glow of his watch face told him it was nine o'clock. In eleven hours, the sea, like a pack of wolves leaping at the ship waiting to devour him, would have its way. No trace of Jack Bonecutter or the poor, beloved Queen Mary would survive.

# Chapter 5

In Panama, Metcalf walked slowly from his living room into the kitchen. He had acquired doctorates in biochemistry, human anatomy and cellular physiology. He was a thinking man.

He never considered himself brave. Never. Yet he knew that, if the Latino got to him first, he would never tell where the briefcase was hidden.

The mysterious Latin man was doubtless aware of the mercenary potential of the chemicals and would auction the weapon to the highest bidder. He would be tenacious, determined.

Back in 1967, Metcalf was sure he had done the right thing, taking the amalgam, literally stealing it from his lab where he was commissioned to work on the top-secret scientific military experiment under the auspices of the United States and British governments.

"Never do anything against conscience, even if the state demands it." Einstein's words haunted him. By developing the mixture against his better judgment, Metcalf had done the exact opposite, and had ever since been paying for it.

After long, agonizing hours of analysis and self-reproach, he decided there was only one viable course: The world would be better off without this weapon. It was then that he took the briefcase, boarded the Queen Mary, and headed for the United States. As he told the FBI agent, he initially planned to drop the briefcase overboard. But something stopped him. In the end, it was as much to save himself as the compound that Metcalf concealed the briefcase and jumped ship in Panama.

In the intervening years, he gradually concluded that the reason he didn't toss the experiment into the ocean was that he was a servant of science. How could he ignore the fact that once one deliberately formed elements into a creation with global consequences, it no longer belonged to you; it belonged to the universe. For better or worse, the compound existed.

Initially, Metcalf had wanted no part of the experiment, but the British and American military convinced him that it was for the "good of his country." Simply the knowledge of such a weapon, they argued, once they were ready to reveal it, ensured that the western super-powers would remain in a position of strength from which to negotiate peace while the Cold War raged, threatening Eastern countries.

Metcalf poured another cup of weak coffee and eased back into a kitchen chair. Until this morning, when he learned of the threat to the Queen Mary, he had been successful in pushing thoughts of the experiment from his mind.

As a scientific experiment, it proved successful well beyond everyone's wildest imaginings. It failed miserably, however, in human terms. Occasionally, he would promise himself that one day he would go to the ship, retrieve the damnable thing, and turn it over to the U.S. Defense Department. But time passed. And now his heart was failing.

Despite his unconscious mind's best efforts, a growing sense of unacknowledged responsibility intermittently returned, and that the amalgam, if unfound, would someday decay. He had no idea how long it would take before that happened. The process could have already begun. At some point, the propellant itself would tend to spontaneously ignite. He had not had time in the lab to adequately address shelf life and the hard questions concerning the compound's ultimate impact, were it allowed to age naturally.

Now, however, the potential for natural decay over a period of years was no longer a factor. The window of opportunity he had in which to deal with the danger had shrunk, a saboteur on the Queen Mary reducing it to hours. Hours he did not have.

Then, of course, there was the man who had assaulted him on the ship. Metcalf recalled the attack vividly. The man assailed him at night in the shadows of the promenade deck. Metcalf, thirty-four years old then and physically healthy, fought wildly, managing to avoid the steel blade as it whipped toward his belly. Twice he was nearly gored.

Then a quick, lateral lunge let him dodge the man's third charge and caught his attacker off guard. The aggressor pitched sideways. Trying to regain balance and avoid the airborne, spinning blade, his assailant stumbled and fell on the knife. Metcalf saw the steel enter the man's face just below the cheek bone, and bury itself to the hilt in the *zygomaticus major*, that muscle which angles the mouth upward when smiling.

Metcalf turned and fled. As he slipped from the ship before first light the next day, he envisioned his attacker's wound, one he knew would forever affect the man's ability to smile, leaving a grotesque, one-sided, painful stretching of lips against a show of teeth.

Metcalf swallowed the last few drops of cold coffee from his mug, and with a shudder tried to rearrange the protrusion that had gradually, over the past few years, developed between his shoulder blades. It was symptomatic of his severe respiratory ailment, emphysema, and its potential for congestive heart failure.

Suddenly he was aware of a din of silence. From the kitchen, he could hear even the slightest sound from the front of the house. But now it was unnaturally quiet; even the quetzals in the guava trees were still. Metcalf winced as another angina pain gripped him. He coughed as the pain increased and stabbed his chest.

This time it was really bad. If only the federal agents from Panama City would hurry. He rubbed his left arm, and simultaneously, a board on the veranda groaned.

# Chapter 6

Captain Benjamin Booker Marshak, Long Beach Police Department, was on his house throne when the phone rang at 8:35 a.m. He was smoking an unfiltered brand and studying the subject of this month's centerfold, a prone, ebon-skinned sister with one hand resting between widely parted, nude thighs. He cursed the phone, which he managed to reach before it woke his wife, and he heard the news about the Queen Mary.

Now he was in one of the two construction mobile offices on the pier beside the threatened ocean liner. Using these as his command post, he quickly completed his on-site assessment, and the evacuation of the ship began.

The First Response units and Major Incident vehicles were arriving. All civilian access, including media entry, to the ship, pier and "A" parking lot was prohibited. The press was all over the situation. By now there was not a city on earth that wasn't carrying the news of Marshak's nightmare.

He jumped as the ship's forward klaxon let loose an ear-shattering blast, announcing nine o'clock. He'd forgotten that the horn sounded every hour. Keyed to lower bass A, it was called "the voice of the Queen Mary." Here beside the ship it was unnerving, suddenly an intolerable assault on Marshak's ears. He grabbed a phone and punched in a number.

"Sergeant Bowyer!" he bellowed. "See that the horn gets the delete key. Now! And for the duration of this crisis." He dropped the phone back into its cradle.

Man, he didn't need this. His twenty years of service had been relatively quiet, his performance as captain of the precinct exemplary. Like his chief, he was tough on all criminals. As he was a fair-minded, second-generation African-American with an African-American-Asian wife, accusations of racial bias seldom plagued his department.

"You carry a big stick," his officers said, referring to the political clout his mixed ethnic background afforded.

Marshak always grinned, his large features loosening into soft folds, and grabbed his crotch in a slick, Michael Jackson move. "You got that right."

Yes, his was a kick-ass department, but he believed solidly in every man's rights under the Constitution of the United States. Unless of course, he was some son of a bitch about to torch the Queen Mary on his watch.

Incendiary bombs. Man! Fire and water was every mariner's nightmare since the Phoenicians set sail in the seventh century. Now they had become his. He remembered when the Queen Elizabeth burned and sank in Hong Kong harbor in 1972. He read about what happened in New York back in the '40s, when the French liner Normandie burned at its mooring. So much water was pumped into her belly that she rolled over and kissed her career goodbye.

"I'll get this guy," Marshak said aloud, "even if I have to storm the ship myself and carry the bastard off by the balls."

If the vessel ignited, the chances of extinguishing the fire with hoses and on-board sprinklers were nill. Her wooden decks, aged and filled with tar strips, would respond to the flames like a hungry infant to its mother's breast. Marshak ran a hand over his head. A few tight, gray-black rings still clung to the rim of his otherwise smooth crown.

"Did you know," he often asked of people who tended to note his increasing hairlessness, "that the head grows bigger as the brain gathers intelligence?"

In fact, he really didn't know if it was true; he never actually read it. But it seemed a fitting prelude to the statement with which he inevitably followed. "As I grow older, I look at it this way: I don't have less hair, just more head."

Flicking a button to respond to his suddenly alive intercom, Marshak thought back to the woman in the centerfold. "What?" he barked in the direction of the speaker.

"Ja…Ja…Jack Bonecutter's agent and his analyst are here, sir," stammered the timorous officer at the desk in the front office. He had been through incidents with his captain before and learned that the heart of a fuzzy teddy bear beat beneath that burly hide, but the bombastic exterior still made him nervous.

Good, Marshak thought. He wanted to talk to those two bozos, get a fix on where this asshole Bonecutter was coming from. "Send them…"

Before he could finish his sentence, the door burst open and a short middle-aged man dressed like a well-heeled cowboy propelled himself toward him. "Captain Marshak? I'm Pete Powers, Jack Bonecutter's literary agent."

He stopped abruptly when the metal tips of his Texas-born boots thudded against the side of Marshak's desk, and turned back toward a thirtyish, gnome-like gentleman who came up beside him.

"This is Jack's therapist, Norman Chaum," Powers went on without losing a beat. "Captain, you've got to let us talk to Jack. We know him. We know what he thinks and how he feels. He's obviously disturbed right now, and what he needs more than anything else is to talk to someone close to him."

"Oh, yeah," Marshak said under his breath. "Since he's holed up on a fuckin' ocean liner that he plans to blow up tonight, along with himself, I'd say he's disturbed, all right." What Marshak said to the men, after compressing his lips for control, was, "How do you do, Mr. Powers, Mr. Chaum?" Without getting up, he offered his hand. "I'm Captain Benjamin Booker Marshak, LBPD. Happy to make your acquaintance."

It was always good to start things off on the right foot. Busy or not, one didn't want to seem inhospitable. "Won't you gentlemen have a seat?"

He indicated two pre-formed plastic, hunter green chairs facing the desk. Chaum took a seat, but Powers paced between the desk and the chairs, running his mouth. "Captain, Jack Bonecutter's not some overly sensitive, high-strung author. He's a sick man who needs to be treated with kid gloves. I'm an agent; kid gloves are my specialty." He paused and leaned over the desk, peering into Marshak's face. "Beyond that, I'm a taxpayer, and as such I've got certain inalienable rights."

"Hold it, Powers," Marshak said, being inhospitable. It was that old my-taxes-pay-your-salary inference that did it. "Let's get this straight: What's really bothering you is that fifteen percent you see going down the tubes."

Marshak immediately regretted the harsh remark. On closer scrutiny, he saw what might be genuine concern in Powers' eyes.

Power's let the comment slide. "The point is, Captain, this whole thing can be stopped right now if you'll only let us talk to Jack. He's a pussycat who wouldn't harm a fly."

Marshak stood up and grinned. Six-two with a large frame, Marshak made another chin as he peered down at Powers. He wanted to quote Mencken: "It is a sin to believe evil of others, but it is seldom a mistake," wanting to add, "In my twenty years in law enforcement I've made few mistakes." But he said only, "Yeah, right."

"Captain Marshak," Norman Chaum, the short, padded, confident man with a full head of hair and sharp, handsome features, said softly, "I can appreciate your position. But if you will only allow me to talk to Jack. He's got a lot bottled up inside. I might be able to make him aware that he can achieve the catharsis, that is, the emotional release, he needs in other ways."

"Phhfft!" Marshak snorted. "I'd say he's emotionally relieving himself pretty nicely out there right now."

Powers stepped in again, switching to a more supplicating tone. "Look, Norm can talk him out of this. I know he can. He's used to dealing with people on the edge."

Marshak walked to the window, giving them his back, and looked out toward the ship. "Ah, yes, the resident shrink, invested with the responsibility for Freudian hocus-pocus."

From his view in the command post near the entrance to the ship, he could see that the evacuation was proceeding in an orderly fashion. There were no signs of panic. In fact, a pocket of chaos at the "A" parking lot entrance seemed to be due not to hurried evacuees but to new arrivals. They were bottom feeders who generally watched reality TV shows and who bee-lined here when they heard the news that the ocean liner might be in delicious jeopardy. What a world.

The pier was cordoned off, and dozens of press vehicles and network news vans circled the perimeter, looking for the best spots in the "B" lot. Marshak heard the phones in the front office ringing incessantly.

Chaum smiled slightly, less than nonplused by Marshak's slur. "I'm a professional psychoanalyst, Captain. I'm not asking you to approve my methods, merely to arrange for me to speak to Jack. My professional opinion is that, in addition to other problems, he still suffers from a form of post-traumatic stress disorder as a result of his experiences in Vietnam in the '70s."

"Oh, great." Marshak turned around and flung up his hands. "As if we haven't all had it up to here with assholes who can't cope and who blame it on their childhoods, their parents, the war. Maybe we should call in Dr. Ruth, who'll no doubt tell us that all of this is due to the fact that Bonecutter failed to masturbate as a child."

He ran a hand over his smooth pate and returned to his desk, lighting up.

Powers waved at the smoke. Inhaling deeply, Marshak exhaled two imperfect rings that wafted in Powers' direction.

"I've smoked all my life," he said slowly. "I'm in perfect health, and my wife of twenty-five years has lungs that inflate like Dizzy Gillespie's cheeks used to." Marshak's brown-eyed gaze stayed on Powers.

"Getting back to the subject at hand," Chaum interjected, "there's also Bonecutter's war wound, which adds to his emotional distress."

"I know about that," Marshak said, on top of things. "I had the Army fax me a copy of his war records."

Chaum was a piranha. "And he is also in transition to mid-life at a time when his marriage is dissolving. His wife..."

"Oh, so now he's having a mid-life crisis, too." Marshak grinned sardonically. "Man, this guy's all fucked up."

"That's just the point," Powers chimed in. "That's why you've got to let at least one of us go aboard, find him and talk to him. I'm his closest friend, for God's sake."

"I don't care if you're his father. You can't go on the ship."

Marshak sighed. If he wanted to get any truly useful input on Bonecutter from these men and get rid of them, he'd better change the tenor of this meeting. He stabbed his generic cigarette into the ashtray.

"Look, fellas, I was out of order. Maybe once we establish communication, I can let you talk to him on the phone. In the meantime, you might as well go home. I've got a job to do. If he wants to off himself in a big way, maybe none of us can stop him. But I am trying. I have men outside who are trained in crisis management. If there's nothing more you can tell me that is helpful..."

"Captain," Chaum said pointedly, "that's what we've been trying to do. Are you familiar with schizophrenia?"

Marshak's eyes flickered skyward. "Split personality. Don't tell me. The voices are making him do it."

Chaum's smile stopped just short of condescending. "In point of fact, multiple personalities are a very rare form of schizophrenia. I'm referring more to a split mind, a splitting from reality, a more common form of the disease, though no less serious. Jack Bonecutter suffers from a severe thought disorder, a serious alteration of perception, emotion and thought, as a result of schizophrenia."

Powers seemed to be into the subject. "Do you think it's genetic in Jack's case?" he asked Chaum. "His father and grandfather were just as obsessed with the Queen Mary as he is."

"Schizophrenia can be heritable," Chaum replied, "but it can also be the result of psychological stress. Or both. You see..."

# Chapter 7

Pete Powers suddenly turned away and walked to the window. The mention of Jack's family made him recall a cross-section of the ship and a photograph of Jack's grandfather he found in Jack's apartment an hour earlier. He had stuffed the two items into a manila envelope. However, since he had left the envelope in the glove compartment of his Porsche when he arrived at the pier, he decided not to mention it.

Powers tuned out Chaum and Marshak as he wondered if there had been a clue to Jack's present behavior that he missed when he stopped by his client's apartment last night.

Jack had been nervous as a bull at a new gate. Maybe, Powers speculated, it was because Lew Blasingdon, CEO of Daystar Studios, impatiently awaited Jack's rewrite of an overdue script.

"Jack," Powers had said, "you know I'm your friend as well as your agent. Your problems are my problems, babe. Tell me, how's the script coming, really?"

Jack hedged. "It's…coming."

"Yeah. Well, maybe I can stall Blasingdon a little longer. Tell you what. I'll go with you to that meeting at the studio in the morning at nine."

Jack did not protest; in fact, he seemed to expect Powers to make this offer, and actually made Powers promise to be at the apartment exactly at eight.

"Okay, I'll be here," Powers agreed. "We'll talk, do coffee before we meet with the big guy."

In a stunning reversal of his usual method of operation, Powers arrived at the Sunset Strip apartment this morning at eight sharp. When Jack didn't answer, Powers let himself in with a key the author had given him a few months earlier. Jack had moved into the apartment when he and his wife separated.

Pete's mind froze for an instant as he read and re-read the note Jack left on the desk, saying he planned to put himself and the famed ocean liner out of their misery.

"Holy shit!"

Pete snatched up the phone and dialed 9ll. It was busy. Was there anyone else he could call? Jack had no family. Melissa, his soon-to-be ex-wife, was on an extended vacation cruising somewhere in the West Indies. The studio, of course. Lew Blasingdon. It was certain that Daystar Studios would want to know anything affecting the future of one of their screenwriters.

Powers knew a good property when he saw one, and the movie Jack was scripting for Daystar looked in every way to him like next summer's smash. The studio's last few releases had gone straight to video, multimillion-dollar special effects' bombs. Jack's poignant, mainstream drama could very well save Blasingdon.

Not that Powers gave a damn about Blasingdon, but maybe the studio's clout could help Powers get on the ship and talk Jack out of the madness he was contemplating.

Loosening the collar of his striped, Garth Brooks-style shirt, he dialed Daystar Studios and read the entire text of Jack's note to the machine that answered Lew Blasingdon's phone. Next he re-dialed 9ll and, getting through, relayed the essence of Jack's words to a jaded, infuriatingly pragmatic woman on the line.

Finally, Powers called a close friend who also knew Jack. Norman Chaum, in-house psychoanalyst for Daystar Studios, had an office in the Daystar tower and was retained to be there for the burgeoning number of stressed-out, Type-A executives. This arrangement saved company time and money, as these administrators no longer had to travel to Beverly Hills' higher-priced shrinks.

Waiting for Chaum to answer, Powers scanned the room. The apartment was neater than usual, neatness with a sense of finality that he hadn't noticed last night. On the desk was an advertisement ripped from the Los Angeles Times, depicting the latest renovations to the Queen Mary. Blatant commercialism, Powers thought. He knew the idea would devastate Jack, whose interest in the ship was gradually reaching obsessive proportions.

On a shelf above the desk was an old photograph of Jack's grandfather, Angus Bonecutter, standing in a section of the Queen Mary's wheelhouse, under construction at the time the photo was taken. Without knowing why, Powers picked it from the shelf, slid it from its frame, and stuck it into a manila envelope from the desk. He tucked it under his arm.

Last night Jack mentioned that the photograph was taken in

the mid '30s, when his grandfather worked on the ship. She was not a name then, but a number: Hull 05340, a skeleton in a misty harbor in Scotland. Jack grew up with stories his grandfather told about her. That was how he came to know every detail of the ship's design.

As years passed, the stories, together with models he constructed and brochures and newspaper clippings he collected, became integral to his sense of family and self. After World War II, his family emigrated from England to the United States, finally settling in Los Angeles, where Jack was born in 1948. They were all dead now; Jack was alone.

"I once made the five-day North Atlantic crossing on her," Jack said last night. "In 1951, when I was three, with my grandfather and parents. It's my earliest childhood memory."

"I don't remember mine," Powers quipped.

Jack seemed not to hear. He said, "That trip was the most exciting yet the most terrifying experience of my life." He turned away, looking at nothing. "Exciting because my grandfather took me up to the crow's nest, that barrel on the mainmast support high above the deck. Terrifying because it was so bizarre and frightening to a three-year-old. He dangled me with his arms outstretched beyond the edge of the crow's nest." Perspiration gathered on his upper lip as he went on.

"I wondered about the ocean. How big was it? Where did the Queen Mary end and the ocean begin? And why did the wind up there above the ship, above the world, it seemed, take the breath from your lungs, press and stifle your mouth and nostrils? I remember looking down and feeling my body freeze with horror. Then I began to scream for grandfather to hold me close, to bring me back from the abyss."

"Jesus." Powers finished his second double scotch. "If that was my experience on the ship, I don't think I'd give a rat's ass about her."

Jack continued to stare into space, his eyes glassy and unanswering, so Powers got up to go. "Terror has its own particular irony," Jack went on. "Once put into perspective, it's comforting, knowing you've faced and endured it. And not only survived it, but played it out, over and over, a thousand times, in your mind and senses, until it became part of you."

He was silent then, as if slowly floating up to the present. He got up and patted Powers on the shoulder. "Don't forget, Pete. Tomorrow morning, eight sharp."

Sadness washed over Powers when he stood in the apartment this morning, remembering. He had suffered dysfunction in his own past. His father left when Pete was just a kid, and he grew up in "La La Land" with few dreams. Before meeting Jack, he was convinced he had to take advantage of everyone in order to survive, to obtain something that seemed due.

Jack had changed that. A writer with great sensitivity, he gave a vulnerable, human edge to even the most terrifying characters he created, and his scripts sold and gave Powers success and self-respect. With these came respectability.

Now, in addition to the million-dollar home, the Porsche, the other trimmings, there were people, from network and studio heads to stars and scenery pushers, who were always in when Pete Powers called.

Still waiting for Chaum to answer the phone, he looked up, and something caught his eye. Tacked to the corkboard above the desk was a sixteen-by-twenty-four-inch cross-section of the Queen Mary. It depicted her interior viewed broadside, details of all inner areas clearly delineated. Penciled alterations indicated the latest structural changes when she was turned into a hotel. Bold red circles were inked in various locations.

Preoccupied, his mind registering the item's importance on a subliminal plane, Powers mechanically removed the tacks from the drawing, folded it, and tucked it into the envelope with the aged photograph of Jack's grandfather.

Finally, Powers heard Norman Chaum murmur a sleepy hello into the phone.

"Listen, Norm, I've some kind of wake-up call for you: Jack Bonecutter's in trouble, big time. I'll explain when I get there. I'll pick you up in ten minutes. We're going to Long Beach."

After hanging up, he crossed to a well-stocked bar and swallowed two fingers of Bell's straight from the bottle; hair of the dog. He bent and wiped away a spot of the amber liquid that spilled onto his genuine reptile boots, straightened and adjusted a silver belt buckle the size of a saucer, and hurried out.

# Chapter 8

In Captain Marshak's mobile office beside the ship, Norm was still pitching his position to Marshak.

"As I said," Chaum concluded, "My diagnosis was subtype undifferentiated schizophrenia. Pete has told me of Jack's occasional lapses into odd speech patterns, something we call clang associations. He rhymes words that make no sense and are totally out of context with the conversation he's engaged in. This is a classic symptom of a severe form of schizophrenia."

Marshak scowled. "Now you're saying the guy talks to himself?" He got up from behind his desk and started toward the door.

"Not exactly. Rhyming words comfort him. They come unbidden to his mind, and sometimes he verbalizes them, wittingly or otherwise."

Marshak noticed that Powers followed him to the door. The police captain opened it and turned back to the therapist. Chaum finally got up, grasped the lapels of his own jacket and leaned forward with an I-know-better-than-you expression.

"Remember, Captain Marshak, that despite your personal opinions on mental illness, you are dealing with a man who has lost contact with reality. He's having delusions about himself and the world in general. Hence, he lives in a mental world quite different from ours. This thing with the Queen Mary is a form of hallucination, the result of disordered thought processes."

Chaum stopped in the doorway and held Marshak's gaze. "Take care, Captain. When the human mind, dealing with a built-in defense mechanism, a psychic compulsion to suppress a traumatic experience or to subconsciously hide from past trauma, suddenly consciously confronts it…well, the first bomb that goes off may be in Jack Bonecutter's head. You may get your explosion before you expect it."

The buzz of Marshak's intercom stung the air, and he stormed back to his desk. "What?"

The voice of the officer at the desk in the outer office quivered as it filled the room. "You…you have a stat call on line one, sir. It's…the Pentagon."

Marshak rubbed a hand through the small patch of hair at his left temple. "The Pentagon? Calling me? You mean THE Pentagon?"

"I believe…yes, that Pentagon, sir."

Marshak punched another button. At the door, Chaum and Powers waited, as if hoping the call might somehow change his decision to ban them from the ship.

Marshak took a few notes as he listened intently. Once he said, "Say *what?*" Finally, he snapped, "Yes, sir," and hung up the phone.

Marshak felt a flush creep up his neck to his face and turn his dark cheeks burgundy. He sank into his chair, suddenly aware that his two visitors were still standing in the doorway.

"Goodbye, gentlemen. Thank you for coming. I'll call you if we need you."

When they did not immediately move, he darted his eyeballs in their direction.

"Goodbye."

Powers mumbled something as they left, leaving Marshak figuring he had not seen the last of them. He swallowed an antacid tablet from a plastic container on the desk and noticed that his heart was pumping hot flashes to his ears.

He couldn't fucking believe it. A colonel no less. A fucking, full-bird army colonel was flying in to take command of his operation.

"We've already spoken to the Governor, the Mayor and your Chief," the Pentagon spokesperson had said, "and you'll be briefed by the colonel on a need-to-know basis. All I can tell you with specificity at this juncture is that national security is at stake, and the United States Army has autonomy in matters of this nature."

"Yes, sir," Marshak had said.

There was more involved than an old ship and a sick dude who wanted to deep-six her.

# Chapter 9

Rufino Jose Quintero was in his late-sixties, of medium height with a thick, powerful body kept in shape by punishing daily exercise. His teeth were strong and even, his dense hair like the mature growth of a chia pet, with gray tufts gaining on their deep brown predecessors.

Quintero was born in the tiny hamlet of Camoruco in the interior of Venezuela in 1947. At age fourteen he left Venezuela, never to return. He traveled as far as limited resources allowed, to Chile, where he took up residence and joined the CLB, the Chileans por Libertad Brigada. The CLB saw to it that Quintero was trained by the best.

In 1972 he reunited with many CLB associates at the Baddawi refugee camp in Lebanon. Here Quintero first took a man's life.

From then on he sold his services as a hired killer to the highest bidder, until, in 1999, he was contacted by a well-organized drug cartel operating behind the facade of a luxurious tourist resort on Pinos Bay, in the Darien jungle of Panama.

The head of this cartel, a man Quintero knew only as el Patrón, had heard of him and employed him exclusively for the past several years. Quintero handled only certain assignments for El Pulpo, his employer's octopus-like network of crime with tentacles in many countries. Quintero's latest kill had been in Loja, Ecuador.

He had just returned home to Pinos Bay, three days before el Patrón called to send him to Contadora.

One of el Patrón's many sources in Panama City informed him of a phone call that would interest Quintero. For many years rumors trickled down from various Washington, D.C. informants about the product of a British-American experiment in biochemical warfare that went missing in 1967.

Now, almost five decades later, the scientist responsible for that product and its disappearance had made a strategic phone call and been located. He was residing almost directly under Quintero's nose.

Today, as he stepped cautiously onto the verandah of the old house on Isla Contadora, he considered this killing with relish, inwardly smiling at the prospect. Quintero, of course, did not smile outwardly, since any such attempt produced an unnatural pulling back of his lips on the right side of his face, resulting in a ghoulish, toothy grin.

Now, at last, Quintero would repay the gringo who was responsible. This prospect was one of the singular pleasures for which he had lived. Slowly he stepped to the screen door of the old man's home. He knew the gringo was alone. His El Pulpo contact had informed him.

Thanks to slipshod governmental security, El Pulpo had penetrated the headquarters of the FBI in Washington and learned of the gringo's phone call minutes after it was completed.

Because Quintero was nearby (Contadora was a short plane ride from Pinos Bay) and because he had a personal stake in the matter, Quintero was given the assignment. In return, he accepted no pay.

"It is my pleasure," he whispered as much to himself as those who'd called him.

He slipped into the living room and slowly made his way toward the kitchen. He would first extract from the scientist where the secret briefcase was hidden, in exactly what part of the ship. Then he would kill him.

The man represented Quintero's one failure. Quintero had been commissioned by the Chileans por Libertad Brigada at the time. His failure on the Queen Mary was Chile's failure, a circumstance that nearly caused his death and was why he left the CLB. If he failed this time, it would be El Pulpo's failure, and el Patrón was not as lax in his discipline as was Quintero's previous employer.

He fully understood how badly they wanted the briefcase. It could mean world domination to whomever possessed it. But none yearned for the conclusion of this matter like Quintero. He had waited more than forty years for this moment.

# The Chemical Factor

# Chapter 10

They scrambled into Lew Blasingdon's office and scurried to be advantageously seated: Directors of Publicity, Public Relations, Legal, Production, and various other departments of Daystar Studios.

Anyone there might have though Lew Blasingdon was Gary Cooper incarnate, with his silver hair and dark horn-rimmed glasses, wearing a neat pin-striped suit. He stood straight and tall behind the desk, silhouetted against partially drawn vertical blinds.

His office was plain and functional. On his desk were a phone/fax, a PC, and several photographs of children, grandchildren, and a salon-tanned wife with expensively sculpted bee-stung lips.

The executives might have described Blasingdon as the picture of reserve and dignity. He made four times their salaries. His four-million-dollar helicopter always remained ready on the helipad two stories above. But the man seemed relaxed to the point of being less than status conscious, as if at his level of stratification there was no necessity for show.

His lean pink face with its tolerant smile furthered that impression. These executives might have thought they heard incorrectly when he addressed them in his smooth, melodious voice.

"I called you all here because I'm happy to announce that one of our scriptwriters has gone berserk and is about to blow up the Queen Mary in Long Beach harbor. I want as much mileage from this serendipitous event as possible.

"And," he went on, "if he somehow gets out of this, I want his ass when it's over. The motherfucker owes me."

The executives were careful to not act surprised by any of this. They knew that Lew Blasingdon's Donna Karin two-thousand-dollar suit never dared wrinkle. They knew that his once-black hair had turned lustrous silver rather than risk his disfavor with a flat, matte gray. His ruddy complexion was not attributable to inner warmth, but to blood pressure pharmaceutically controlled but volatile. The perpetual smile that strangers read as tolerant was proof of the depth of his determination to publicly appear so.

Questions piled upon questions, from the group in his office.

"What writer?"

"Have the police been notified?"

"Do you think he means it?"

"Why the Queen Mary?"

Some, like Blasingdon, never cramped by the tyranny of conscience, began to contemplate the movie that could be made, and who was available to direct.

Blasingdon sat down at his desk and held up a hand with slender fingers and subtly manicured nails. "This is the message that was relayed to me in my car on the way in, patched through from my machine here." He tapped a button on the fax phone, and Pete Powers' unsteady voice was heard reading Jack Bonecutter's message.

When it was completed, Blasingdon nodded. "Now you know as much as I do. Assume the police have been notified. Your single consideration should be how we can milk this thing from every conceivable angle, no matter how remote. I'd like to see our man draw this out as long as possible, take hostages, make public threats, build public interest."

He cleared his throat and nodded in the direction of his publicity head. "If there's anyone nearby with a video camera who catches any of this, I want his or her tape, no matter what the cost, before the FOX news hounds get hold of it. Questions?"

Maggie Culina, Vice President of Post-production, ventured, "It sounds like Jack Bonecutter needs help. Most of us know him. Isn't there anything we could do to help…"

Blasingdon interrupted her by standing, and gestured for an all-rise. "I have another meeting." He checked his watch. "It's nine-fifteen. We'll meet here again at ten-thirty. I'll want your suggestions, legal considerations, the works."

His minions slowly filed from the office.

By the time the door closed behind them, Blasingdon already knew what he was going to do. He planned to wait for their input. Let them earn their preposterous salaries. He earned his. He worked hard at making millions, and even harder at making it appear that those millions were immaterial to him.

He replayed Powers' message, and thanked the fates that it

was not his responsibility to find Bonecutter and the bombs. Blasingdon had taken the Queen Mary tour on several occasions when certain of his bourgeois relatives came to town and needed to be entertained.

Being slightly familiar with the ship, he thought of thousands of places where Bonecutter could hide, and millions of nooks and crannies into which the explosives could be secreted.

# Chapter 11

Agent Susan Koski ran with long easy strides, breathing the fresh morning air. Six-thirty a.m. and the streets of Reno were already beginning to fill with early morning traffic. Her cell phone chirped and she slowed to flip it open.

"On your fourth mile yet, Koski?" It was her boss, Frank Heeley.

"Almost at the end of the fifth and final. What's up?"

"Plenty. I want you down at the military section of Reno Airport ASAP. Report to the C.O. He'll fill you in. Pack a small bag. You're going for a fast ride in a small plane. I'll be in touch."

The line went dead. Koski increased her pace.

# Chapter 12

Sharp, nauseating pain grabbed Gordon Metcalf's heart and squeezed.

"Oh God!"

He slumped against the table. This time it was much worse than before. This time...in some dimension of his stuttering senses, he heard footsteps in the house, approaching the kitchen...the angina struck again, and he clutched his left arm, his chest. Breath left him. He looked up the moment the stranger entered the room. No, not really a stranger.

Quintero's eyes glistened. His half-smile twisted into a grimace as he reached into the sheath that held the unusual blade that was his signature. Metcalf was ten years older than Quintero, stoop-shouldered, tall but thin as a heron, his skin paler than white. The scientist knew that this time there would be no contest.

Pain blurred Metcalf's vision, yet he was able to make out the glint of steel.

"Finally, gringo."

Quintero's thick, powerful body inched forward as if this was a fortunate day, this minute too sweet to hurry. Metcalf assumed his killer would use the blade first as persuasion, to extract information about the briefcase's location, then do the final deed slowly.

Grasping the knife handle, which itself was noble, cut from the beak of *el pico de pez espada*, the mighty swordfish of the sea, Quintero's face suddenly took on a contemplative look, as though he were imagining the blade slithering first into his victim's gut, in and out, over and over, leaving Metcalf to die in as many parts of his body as possible.

"Forgive me, Padre, for I have sinned," Metcalf easily imagined Quintero meekly confessing tomorrow. "A man with a suitcase filled with bad scientific magic sought to murder many thousands of innocents. It was my place, my duty, to kill him, Padre."

Then Metcalf wheezed and doubled over, struggling for a single breath.

Metcalf could already feel the death of his organs. Oblivious to any human presence now, he was cosmically aware of oxygenated blood returning from his lungs to the left atrium of his heart, where a valve opened, allowing the flow to enter the left ventricle, which prepared to contract, but paused.

"No!" Quintero leapt beside him. "No!"

He grabbed the front of Metcalf's shirt and pulled the limp man to his feet as if, though there were others on the ship in California that he would kill before this day closed, only this death was *muy importante*.

"*Basta!*" Quintero screamed.

Metcalf's body let go and slumped before Quintero's blade

could find it, his last thought of the Devil's crucible, and his dying wish that somehow someone would find it in time to redeem him.

# Chapter 13

Marshak heard a commotion in the outer office of his command post, but kept his eyes on the window as a wide, squat, Army UH-1 Iroquois helicopter, better known as a "Huey," thundered in his direction. Muscular and minatory, the olive-brown craft thumped over the water, flying low and slow, allowing full view of waist gunners on either side of its open doors.

"Definite command presence," Marshak thought aloud, turning his attention to a chopper from a local television station, circling like a blue-fly above the Queen Mary. "You're about to get your marching orders," Marshak mumbled in the fly's direction.

The United States Army would soon remind the media insect that air space above the ship was restricted within three miles, altitude two thousand feet.

The floor of the command post shuddered with deafening vibration as the Huey swept past the TV chopper at six hundred feet. The media pest, getting the word, turned tail and left the restricted area.

After one more menacing pass over the ship, the Huey put

down on the helipad adjacent to the parking area opposite Carnival Cruise Lines lot "D," bordering Ocean View Avenue and the exit ramp from the Harbor Freeway. Within minutes a field-uniformed mini-Schwarzkopf marched into Marshak's office, flanked by two crisp aides.

"Colonel J. Manley Beard, United States Army Rapid Deployment Forces," he said and gave Marshak's hand one solid jolt.

He was a short, neat man with buzz-cut, carrot-red hair dappled with gray. His eyes were small and very blue, clear as a boy's, his face emanated straightforward expression. He automatically seated himself behind the desk Marshak considered his own.

"We understand that evacuation of the ship is nearly complete and proceeding in textbook fashion. Good work, Captain. We like that."

Marshak was silent. *And if we don't, tough titty.*

"We've been in touch with FEMA and the Office of Homeland Security, the Navy, Air Force. The CAB, FAA and NTSB have assured us of their full cooperation, if such should become necessary." He turned and gave the room a quick, but thorough appraisal.

"We'll use this office while we're here at Com Cen, Captain. The outer office is being equipped with computers, television and radio equipment, to be interfaced with the ship's existing security system. We'll have a state-of-the-art digital umbilical cord, so to speak, tying us into the ship's internal closed-circuit communication network."

So that was the buzz of activity Marshak heard in the outer office; his command post was already being converted into Com-Cen.

"In fact," Beard went on, "the first areas of this floating hotel will be beaming back to monitors here very shortly. Miller and Nakamura," he indicated his two aides, who silently nodded and adjourned to the outer office, "should get us clear, sharp definition in both color and black and white."

He quickly whisked Marshak's overflowing ashtray from the desktop and tossed it into the small "round file" in the kneehole of the desk, never missing a beat in his speech.

"Broadcast quality digital video will be on continual 'record' to relay anything they see on the ship." He stood and reached for Marshak's hand again. "Between us, Captain, this Bonecutter fellow and the whole business scares the living hell out of me."

Marshak noted that he abandoned the royal pronoun for this little heart-to-heart.

"I know you don't like it, Captain. Certainly, I don't enjoy it. But, in a sense, it's war, isn't it? And one doesn't expect to enjoy war, does one? In a war, neither side knows who will win, only that their job is to kill people."

Marshak tipped him a bogus "right on" and was silent. *No fucking kidding! You must be some kind of fucking Rapid Deployment genius.*

"However," Beard added, "we're going to win this one. And we won't concern ourselves as to who gets the credit, will we? So long as we get the job done."

Beard gripped Marshak's right shoulder with his free hand.

"Right, Captain?"

Marshak felt heat rush up to his ears and wished he could control the flush of frustration and anger that he knew was evident. But he had to stifle it, at least for now. It looked like he was going to be stuck babysitting this self-aggrandizing Army egoist for a while.

"Right," he finally replied, and was released from the colonel's grip. "We still call the Queen Mary a ship, sir. Not a hotel."

"Whatever. We'll need to talk in a few minutes," Beard said, checking all the drawers of the desk to make certain they were empty.

Turning and heading for the door, Marshak said, "We'll take the smaller office, the one down the hall adjoining your outer office. Sir."

When Marshak got to the diminutive office, workmen were busy connecting his phone, and there was a note on the otherwise barren desk, stating that a manila envelope addressed to him had been left with the guard at the "A" parking lot gate. It would be delivered to his office presently.

He called the guard and learned that the envelope was left earlier by exiting Hollywood agent Pete Powers. What the fuck could that be? Well, Marshak didn't have time for Powers or his mystery envelope right now.

# Chapter 14

Clinging to the old wooden ladder in the dark shaft, Bonecutter could make out faint syllables as the ship's PA system lisped the repeated evacuation order. It instructed personnel and guests to leave the ship immediately, giving no explanation and emphasizing the fact that there was no imminent danger.

To relieve stress on any particular part of his body or limbs, Bonecutter had turned around, his back now facing the ladder, heels downward for balance, dug into position on the horizontal rung. His arms encircled the two-by-four vertical sides of the ladder, using them like suspenders to prevent him from the unthinkable: toppling to his death before the appointed time.

He had chosen eight p.m. for a reason. To be sure it was dark, precluding his seeing the ocean from the chart room above, where he planned to be at detonation. He preferred that the wolf waves not be part of his final vision.

His eyes were closed, and he re-envisioned the sight that had brought him here this day. He allowed that those who owned her had kept the ship in excellent superficial condition. Glossy new red-and-black paint adorned her three smokestacks. The bulk of her hull was painted black, except for the marine red anti-rust area at the waterline and the wide band of white that covered the exterior of the top three decks: the sports deck, the sun deck, and the promenade deck.

But that slick new facade was the only virtue Bonecutter ascribed to those who currently possessed her. She was landlocked and abused, profaned and exploited. Portside and amidships, elevated walkways and up and down escalators leading to the gangways marred the perspective of her beauty.

Sprawling, spider-like scaffolding was continually needed to maintain stairways, handicapped access, additional restrooms and the other trappings of tourism. They all scarred her former majesty. Constant refurbishing and renovating to accommodate paying guests gutted her authenticity.

Bonecutter deeply resented the way she had been handled. Every decision in her past should have been undertaken glacially, and only those intimately familiar with her past should be allowed to tamper with her future. Well, her future was his now.

When he had arrived earlier with his carryon containing the bombs, he was not challenged. He might have been a terrorist, but security personnel only randomly checked belongings; he paid his admission and walked past the checkpoint with a nod and a smile.

On the escalator, his gaze fell on the wooden railing of the promenade deck where a long line of dew had gathered and become moist jewels that winked in a sudden shaft of sunlight. Swallowing against a sense of sadness, he stepped onto the elevated amidships walkway, turned right and went down the stairs to the lower decks.

He began at the stern, the planned location of his first incendiary device being one of the two sites where once the mighty engine rooms were located, the very bottom of the aft portion of the ship. The engine rooms once housed four-thousand-horsepower steam turbines that propelled her through the stormy North Atlantic in excess of thirty knots.

It was early, not even eight a.m. when he came aboard, yet tourists by the dozens were everywhere, chattering excitedly in various languages. Whatever happened to English? He might have been Magellan putting into an inhospitable port.

During the next forty-five minutes, Bonecutter worked his way forward. He stealthily found eight of the predetermined locations and covertly secreted an incendiary explosive in each. They now rested ominously in the old engine room, Ye Olde Bakery Shoppe, the QM cinema, the wedding chapel, the QM History Museum, the long table in the Country Cottage Room, the Trafalgar Square gift shop, and a first-class stateroom suite on the promenade deck near the bow.

His two remaining units were to be placed in the Churchill Lounge beneath the navigational bridge, and in the signals and flag cabinet in the wheelhouse section of the bridge itself.

When he had entered the lounge, he counted less than a dozen people, most focused on the surrounding glass windows facing the foredeck, and preoccupied with the panoramic view of the bay and the gathering gray clouds above it. Gingerly fingering the two explosive incendiaries in his pants pocket, he walked to the far end of the bar.

"Water, please," he told the young waiter who raised his head and eyebrows in receipt of the order.

Fighting impatience, Bonecutter was forced to wait for the right time to position the explosive. Precious minutes ticked away.

He had finished his water when a waitress came up and, leaning against the bar, put in an order for a Bloody Mary. While her body shielded his hands from the patrons' view, Bonecutter slipped the next-to-last nest from his pocket and pressed the wax adhesive to the underside of the thick, polished mahogany lip of the bar.

As he walked out, he sighed with relief. Only one bomb left, and that would be placed in the flag cabinet in the wheelhouse. Then he would enter the adjoining chart room and open the trap door to the shaft below the chart table. He slid the remote firing unit into his shirt pocket and headed for the staircase leading to the bridge.

# Chapter 15

Bonecutter felt inspirited, alive for the first time in months. He knew that the wail of sirens swelling in the distance announced the arrival of ambulances, SWAT teams, probably a Haz-Mat van, and other emergency vehicles.

As he climbed the stairs, he glanced up and his vision was captured by the crow's nest perched more than halfway up the forward main mast. When out at sea, all the sailors felt sorry for the whoever was assigned lookout duty there. When the bitter North Atlantic winds raged around the vessel, a man could turn to ice in ten minutes or less. A shudder passed over Bonecutter, as if a cold, metallic ribbon was drawn across his spine.

Four decades earlier, Bonecutter's grandfather had taken him high above the deck and into that round metal lookout, placing three-year-old Jack on the rim with his stubby legs dangling against the side, air alone between them and the sea. At first he felt no fear. He laughed and pointed to the sun, a giant peach sinking fast into a gray sea, much larger than he imagined and whose surface rippled with gold.

From down on the deck, the ship was so huge, unending and immense that the distant waters would never see a three-year-old above it. Yet high in the crow's nest, little Jack saw it was the sea that was immense and never-ending, looking like a pack of wolves constantly leaping up at the ship, threatening to drag her down to destruction.

With the sun rapidly descending, Jack soon could not distinguish where the vessel ended and the pack began. He quickly switched his vision back to the horizon just as a final gleam of sunlight blinked and faded. Thin drafts of icy air rose around him and he shivered. Suddenly he wanted to get down, and he turned his upper body back toward his grandfather, outstretching pleading arms.

"Whee," Grandfather cried and scooped him up into his arms with such swift strength that Jack let out a little shriek of startled, breathless shock.

At first he did not know what happened or where he was. He thought he was riding high against his grandfather's chest, but his body lost its weight and he seemed to be floating in space. Then he knew he was on his back, his head draped over one of his grandfather's arms, his legs over the other.

"Whee," sang Grandfather again, extending his arms far out over the edge of the crow's nest and swinging young Jack back and forth, back and forth, until Jack's eyes dizzied and hurt.

The wind roared past his stinging ears and stole the breath from his chest. What felt like a gale pressed against his face and forced his nostrils shut. He felt nauseous, giddy, at the mercy of great, uncontrollable gulps, his eyes running tears, his nose bubbling with mucus. Kicking his feet and flailing his arms did nothing to stop the terror; in fact, he felt certain he would fall.

On and on it lasted, the old man's voice like eerie music that the child heard but did not hear, repeating, "Whee, little Jack, whee!"

Finally, his child's heart beating thunderously, he found himself again against his grandfather's chest, back on deck, trying to close his mouth against a scream, seeing his own terror in his parents' faces as they raced to him.

For years Bonecutter tried to push thoughts of that day away. Ultimately, he found that reliving was a tactic, not of forgetting, but of forbearing. Yet it left his feelings confused. Abused and violated, yet cuddled and loved, driven to strike out while compelled to submission. And there was no one to blame.

He loved his grandfather. Had they not gone to the edge of life together and survived? Did they not have a bond stronger than death?

Balancing on the ladder in the shaft below the chart room, Bonecutter yet again paid the price of remembering.

The shrinking feeling that was the precursor of what he had come to think of as a "spell," began to tighten against his temples. The roar of air in the shaft pounded in his head and the involuntary growl that gurgled in his throat like deformed dulcimer music escalated to a din that pressed unbearably against his eardrums. He could not think clearly. He felt his eyes roll around in their sockets.

Losing the fight for control, his mind went outside his head, taunting its empty shell, and yet the pressure built, his head pulsating. Releasing one arm from its grip around the vertical post of the ladder, he slammed his fist once, twice, against his forehead.

"No! No!" he rasped.

But it went on and on. Finally, gradually, the pressure slipped away, and the only thought he could collect from the dizzying vortex in his mind was childish and disjointed.

"Tinker bell, Tinker bell, go to hell, you smell," he heard himself say in a foreign, lilting tone.

# Chapter 16

Seated beside the pilot in a helicopter sporting army colors and flashing toward San Pedro, Joseph Falk thrashed through thoughts of his earlier phone conversation with Frank Heeley. Falk's new bureau chief tended to overstate a situation. This, it seemed, was not one of them.

"Back in the 1960s," Heeley had said, "in an experiment never written up in any journals or disclosed beyond a small circle of high-level British and American scientists and statesmen, a powerful step had been taken. Dr. Metcalf had built into his infusion the chemical means by which a vital human gene, p53, would mutate.

"Gene mutation is a molecular change in the structure of a single gene inside a cell. Mistakes in DNA replication can cause mutation, some of them inheritable changes. But the application of chemical agents, called mutagens, induce or at least greatly increase the rate of mutation. Depending on the mutagens, it could happen over a lifetime or immediately.

"For purposes of his experiment, change was dubbed 'lethal' if it eventually resulted in the death one way or another. Certain chemicals in Metcalf's witch's-brew mixture killed immediately. Other's took their time or simply increased overall likelihood or efficacy.

"The mixture was developed for military use in war, so a propellant was added to disperse and disseminate the lethal properties into the air. There were other chemical additives, like a binding agent and preservatives. And a retrovirus with a natural homing instinct to find its way into the exposed's stem cells in the bone marrow.

"Even worse was what Metcalf resisted including, but upon which the military insisted. Like a number of mutagens. One, for example, an industrial waste product, did two things: when it moved into a cell, it mutated the p53 gene, a critical growth-regulator. This gene normally attached itself to a cell's DNA at specific locations, and bound onto questionably activated genes whose proteins controlled cell division."

Falk had taken copious notes and studied them carefully. He had difficulty writing, as Heeley quickly became breathless, and began to talk faster but more softly.

"A mutated p53 gene lacks the ability to bind to the DNA and thereby fails to turn on the gene involved in turning off cell proliferation. Therefore, not only would the cell experience frenzied, uncontrollable growth, as do cancerous cells, but the mutated gene also would induce the production of an enzyme rendering other toxins in the cell more potent.

"Thus, the mutated p53 gene would result in death by multiple mutagen-caused diseases. And if it did not kill directly, it ended up contaminating the individual's gene pool for generations."

Falk said what Heeley was about to say. "A cloud of these

chemicals released over California by the explosion when fire reached the briefcase would start a chain reaction of death and deformity, moving rapidly, threatening populations across the Western United States for decades."

"Yes," replied Heeley simply.

Falk had been held up at Van Nuys airport, a congressman having commandeered the chopper originally scheduled for Falk, so he began his search of the Queen Mary forty-five minutes later than planned.

A cool slither of water dropped onto his hand and he reached up and swiped at an errant strand of still-wet, chestnut hair dangling over his forehead. After Heeley had hung up, Falk had only enough time to jump in and out of a cold shower, dress, and strap on his 9 mm Beretta before the car arrived to take him to the airport. Now he shivered, as much from the overwhelming weight of his mission as from the dampness of his hair and the cool morning air.

On Heeley's orders, he advised no one of his assignment. He couldn't phone Koski. She was on a routine assignment in Reno, doing timed surveillance on a racketeer the Bureau was interested in. Agents watched the suspect in stages, each assigned to a particular part of his day. Knowing Special Agent Susan Koski, Falk felt sure she was bored to tears. Here in Long Beach was the kind of assignment she craved. And speaking of cravings, he missed her.

Joe's senses suddenly filled with her essence. He loved the fresh, lingering scent of Savon Doux Place des Lices Pivoine, the peony soap with which she bathed, but it was her natural scent he most savored. And the tactile silkiness of her hair that complimented the translucence of her skin that glowed with pale peach undertones. Beyond the physical and emotional response her mere presence evoked in him, she was simply comfortable to be around.

Her IQ slightly exceeded his own, something he alternately admired and resented, which occasionally caused some friction between them. When there was time and they got together, they usually talked a lot. But even Koski's silences were good company.

To Falk's way of thinking, too many of today's young women were tough, sneering, ball-busting wonder women who had bought into their own publicity. He was weary of the stereotype, of faces afraid to register primness or frailty.

He liked that he had witnessed both in Koski. On her first assignment, he saw her kill a man, then momentarily fall to pieces, like a broken sparrow, from the heart-wrenching pain of that ungodly act.

Joe straightened and looked out of the chopper at the landscape that was fast-reeling itself under the nose of the aircraft, and nudged his thoughts back to his phone call from Heeley.

Once Falk knew the facts of the situation, Heeley didn't have to spell out the consequences of failure. The irony was that Jack Bonecutter himself could not be aware of the real horror he would unleash if the Queen Mary exploded in flames.

The poor, sick bastard had no idea of the chain reaction his personal vendetta against those who enslaved his ship would cause because of a mixture of chemicals fashioned into a biochemical weapon of war and hidden aboard the ship long ago.

"Thousands, maybe millions of unsuspecting people are in imminent danger of exposure to the deadly chemicals," Heeley had explained before their phone conversation ended. "And you are their only hope of survival, Falk."

Falk was ordinarily an optimistic person, but he knew he needed all the help he could get on this one. "You said that the briefcase containing this chemical fusion was put on the Queen Mary in 1967 by the scientist who created it. And you said that you have located this man in Panama, right?"

"Well, yes."

"And you'll get the exact location of the briefcase from him and relay it to me, right?"

"Right. And we will tell you, the minute we know…"

Falk was uneasy about putting stock in Heeley's words when he let his sentences dangle in that fashion, but he had no choice other than trusting Heeley now.

"I'm no chemist, Frank," Falk had said, "but I understand basic human cellular physiology. Tell me again what these gene-altering chemicals do."

"Here's the way it was put to me by a scientist who knew something about this experiment," said Heeley. "When exposed, cells making up those tissues and organs would be overrun by these pernicious compounds. Depending on the degree of exposure, they'd kill their hosts immediately or kill them slowly over time, or mutate their genes irreversibly, altering the entire protein-producing mechanism of their bodies and affecting them and their offspring for generations."

"Is there anything you haven't told me that could possibly make this situation worse?" Falk asked.

"It's December, and the freakin' Doppler radar shows a red storm cell offshore that's being driven east in the Pacific by thirty-mile-an-hour-plus winds with gusts expected to reach seventy miles per hour by nightfall.

"The cloud that would be generated and rise as a result of Bonecutter's incendiary bombs exploding and igniting the hidden container of toxic chemicals would destroy all human life within an undetermined radius in the way I just described. And, this is the worst part, the wind would at the very least, carry that toxic cloud inland, over all of Long Beach, a city of approximately 71,000 people, and from there LA and beyond."

Falk experienced an icy dread. "Frank," he asked, "what degree of exposure does it take?"

"As little as three hundredths of a milligram inhaled would be lethal. Those who do not die instantaneously will see their cells, diseased by mutagens, begin to grow uncontrollably. As I understand it, one of the many deadly aspects of this mixture is that it contains a retrovirus designed to find its way into the bloodstream and, ultimately, to the stem cells in the bone marrow itself."

"God! So not only will cancerous cells form, and proliferate, there would be a total breakdown of the immune system as well."

"Correct. Death would be a certainty once membranes

strangling the lungs triggered respiratory paralysis."

It was Falk's nature to grasp at straws. "Frank, wouldn't at least some of the elements in this stuff have a half-life of some specific duration? You said the container was hidden on the ship in the late 1960s. Wouldn't some properties have altered, maybe even been rendered ineffective to some extent by now?"

"I asked the same question, and was told that, contained as these properties supposedly are, in a hermetically sealed container inside a reinforced steel briefcase, they could probably remain unchanged and lethal for a hundred years."

Falk's thoughts darkened. Chemicals, it seemed, were to be the theme of his day. Wasn't that a perversion of exactly what chemotherapy was? A bombardment of chemicals into one's body to kill the cancer cells. Falk fumed as he pondered the scientist in Panama. What kind of monster would concoct such a mixture?

The helicopter banked left and descended to five hundred, then four hundred feet. Falk looked out at the western sky, which was slate gray with thunderheads like fluffy sheep piling up against one another. Wind ruffled the sea like the feathers of a herring gull.

A storm was forming, headed in the same direction as he. A light fog swirled beneath them, broken and web-like, then Falk caught the smell of salt, fish, diesel fuel and humanity, and glimpsed the Queen Mary below.

Viewing the ship's three monumental smokestacks, he thought she was majestic, even in captivity. A shrine to lost opulence, to the pampered leisure of pre-World War II transatlantic ocean voyaging. In the more than sixty years since her maiden voyage in 1936, she had hosted now-deceased presidents, dignitaries and other celebrities from all over the world. Churchill once held press conferences and over-drank in her Art Deco bar.

Falk imagined her at sea, the soft wash of water caressing her bow. But now she was permanently dry-docked in Long Beach California. Maybe he understood some of what Jack Bonecutter must feel. The moan of her old wooden decks could be construed as a cry for help, for peace, as tourists who lacked the sense of history to thrill at her legacy trekked through her. They sought the only prize a desensitized, under-educated, violence-overloaded, flagging civilization could conceive: ghosts in her galleys.

Falk sighed deeply, sighting the large, blue X on the helipad located on a raised platform just east of the outer parking lot. Three hundred feet away were two construction trailers that appeared to be a command post, a buzz of police activity around them.

The pilot roared toward the helipad without any sign of decreasing his speed. Falk turned to him.

"What's up?" His voice crackled into the pilot's helmet.

"Up, sir?" The pilot asked.

"The helipad." Falk pointed as the large X vanished beneath them and was quickly left behind. He had expected to deplane there.

"My orders are to deposit you on the ship, sir. Astern, on the sun deck, next to the Ye Olde Bakery Shoppe, sir."

"On the…"

Falk had assumed he would first meet at dock HQ with the colonel Heeley had mentioned. He shrugged. Probably there was nothing Colonel Beard could add to those professional, precise orders Heeley had given Falk on the phone: "Until we get a location from the scientist, all I can tell you, Joe, is to get on board and follow your instincts."

Falk checked his watch. It was ten forty-five. Was it really less than two hours ago that he spoke to Heeley? It seemed more like days ago when Heeley solemnly pronounced, "Joe, you understand that at this point we can't let the public, the media, or even the police, know the truth.

"That would open up a can of worms we definitely don't want opened. Especially since we failed to get our hands on the briefcase back in '67. As far as everyone is concerned, you're there only to locate Bonecutter and his bombs."

Heeley lowered his voice conspiratorially. "And, of course, a man is a lot easier to find than a briefcase, so your primary search will be for Bonecutter. If you happen to get your hands on the briefcase first, before you're able to apprehend Bonecutter or locate his bombs, get the hell off the ship." Even the Bureau viewed the old girl and the schizoid who obsessed over her as expendable.

As the chopper continued to descend, Falk tried to concentrate on strategy, or his lack thereof. He reminded himself that uphill battles were his specialty. Falk had learned early on that he alone was accountable for his actions, which made him a tough, independent competitor.

On the other hand, finding an unbalanced man and his bombs and a one-foot-square briefcase hidden on an ocean liner nearly a thousand feet long and twelve stories high was not going to be easy. And time was moving on relentlessly.

Heeley had held out one ray of hope: the chemist in Panama who originally hid the briefcase on the ship. The only clue Heeley ascertained from the Bureau agent who spoke to the man was that he had hidden it somewhere no one would find it.

"The scientist is sick, old, maybe even feeble-minded," Heeley muttered, "but as soon as we have him, we'll have an answer for you, Joe."

# Chapter 17

Falk was given exactly four seconds to jump from the helicopter onto the sun deck astern, before the pilot's collective pitch change required a burst of power, and the chopper lifted and disappeared over the bay.

Quickly sighting his cover, Falk bolted across the exposed deck toward amidships, vaulting over a long, low bench, running full-tilt, hoping the bomber was not nearby.

Reaching Ye Olde Bakery Shoppe, he rammed a shoulder against the push-bar door and burst in, turning and slamming his back to the wall just inside. He scanned the room. He had worn one of his weighted jackets: two small, flat weights like those used in shower curtains were sewn inside the left front lower lining. The weights flipped it out and away if he were required to simultaneously twist, bend to become the smallest possible target, and reach for his holstered Beretta.

The precaution of inserted weights could save a second in opening his jacket, and therefore his life. He instinctively felt, more than saw or heard movement, as his weapon cleared leather.

"Don't shoot me!"

The voice came from behind the coffee counter, just below a sign on the wall that read "Espresso, Freshly Baked Pastries, Desserts & Other Sweets."

A sensational, tanned blonde with brilliant green eyes and a smile that certainly could be described as sweet stood up, empty palms uplifted in his direction.

"Koski!"

"Hi, Joe." Her tone was almost timorous.

He could not believe it. His heart seemed to float at the sight of her, as always. But she shouldn't be here. "What are you... how did you get here?"

Susan Koski rolled her eyes, swung her petite body around the counter, and sauntered toward him. The timid demeanor disintegrated, replaced by her usual confidence, which presently included an edge of sarcasm.

"Glad to see you, too."

He watched her take note of his charcoal blazer and black pants; then she looked down at her own outfit—jeans, oversized beige sweater, and J. Crew jacket, white socks and high-tops.

"My invitation said casual," she quipped, handing him a Bluetooth phone ear bud. She indicated the earpiece. "Cutting-edge, latest issue from Quantico."

She pulled back her hair and revealed a similar, small flesh-toned earpiece fitted snuggly into her ear. "The microphone is built in and picks up our voices from vibrations in our heads."

Falk didn't like this development one iota. This mission was dangerous enough for one, let alone two. One person might escape Bonecutter's notice, but he would surely spot two. He held up a hand to signal her to silence and went to the window. It looked like a ghost ship out there; the stern section quiet and totally devoid of movement, indicating that the evacuation was no doubt complete, and that Bonecutter probably was not in the immediate vicinity. Falk re-holstered his weapon and ran a hand through his rich brown hair.

"What are you doing here, Koski? How did you get aboard?"

Her full lips pouted. "Last question first. I got here ahead of you and the ship was still being evacuated, so I played the part of an official herding the people ashore. No time for amenities, I guess."

She shrugged and continued, "Heeley pulled me off the Reno surveillance gig. Said he had talked to you, maybe twenty minutes earlier. Said his intention was to fly me here where I would meet at dock HQ with the local yokels and this Army Colonel Beard. I was to stand by in case you needed two more hands. And, by that time, he would have word from agents in Panama as to the location of the briefcase, which I, being the only other person to know about said briefcase, would pass on to you."

She paused to take a breath. Falk was silent, wondering when her needle would hit empty.

"So," she continued, "he sent a jet-powered chopper out of Reno-Tahoe to fly me here, which took less than forty minutes. I should have been here after you, except I heard you got held up at Van Nuys Airport. Just a few moments ago, Heeley called me at headquarters dockside, and said I should get aboard at the stern. Like I said, I played an official evacuator."

Falk had to interrupt. "So Heeley figures I can't handle this one on my own. Is that the bottom line?"

"No. It's not that at all."

"It's not? What is it, then? You tell me."

She straightened, and her glowing green eyes pierced his. "That's what I'm trying to do." She paused and sighed. "I was told to tell you that, unfortunately, we won't get any help from the scientist in Panama. When the agents arrived at his home on Contadora Island, he was dead; stabbed several dozens of times, although it appears as if he died of a heart attack before the stabbings."

"Jesus!"

Falk eased back against the wall. As Koski approached him, he caught the warm aroma of peony soap on her skin and the fresh scent of her hair.

Her tone was softer and more empathetic. "Heeley decided that, given the new circumstances, you might appreciate an additional someone to help you in the hunt. So here I am."

She combed a hand through her thick blond hair, and it furrowed between her slender fingers, then fell back into place.

"So, where do we begin, Joe?"

He looked down from his six-foot height at her five-one, a tad over a hundred pounds. A deep sigh washed over him. He placed a hand on her shoulder and let it slowly slide down her arm to her warm hand, where their fingers entwined.

"I am glad to see you," he said truthfully, quickly looking away, avoiding those eyes he could so easily get lost in.

A brief touch was all there was time for. That seemed to be

their lot in life: jumping from one assignment to another, never having enough time to properly explore some of the deeper, important conversations of life.

"Look," he said, moving away from her spell. "Here's how I see it. Logically, if I were this guy, Bonecutter, and I was obsessed with the ship and planned to die with her tonight, I'd feel like I was in charge of her now. Like, finally, I was the captain of her fate. Where would the captain be?"

Koski raised her eyebrows, as if she had not already thought of it. "On the bridge."

"Right. But there's no good place for a man to hide on the bridge, as far as I know. When the police and security personnel evacuated the ship, surely they checked the bridge, the wheelhouse, that entire area. Nevertheless, I think he'd be as close as possible to the navigational nerve center of the ship, possibly positioned to move to the bridge once darkness closed in."

"Assuming that's true, giving us his possible general location, we're left with the bombs and the briefcase."

"The location of the bombs is something we'll have to hope we can persuade Bonecutter to tell us, if and when the time comes. As to the briefcase, which is our secondary, but more important mission, if we find Bonecutter and his babies, it won't matter where the case is, at least for the moment, and that'll become another story."

"I have a hunch," Koski said.

*Female intuition*, Falk thought disparagingly. Even so, one had to consider it's origin. If it was Koski, it was never without merit. He and Koski had worked together on one assignment in the past year, the serial killings in Nevada and California. Koski's hunches had proven generally accurate throughout; he had to give her that. He decided to project an interested look.

"What hunch is that?"

"The scientist, Metcalf, kept a low profile when he took that voyage back in 1967, so he obviously was not in a stateroom. He stayed hidden. His access was limited to places where a lot of people congregated where he blended in unnoticed or places where there wasn't anyone around, where others could or would not go, where he'd not be seen."

Falk raised his eyebrows and gave her a slightly impatient bottom line gesture with his hand.

"My guess is someplace like the gym. Or, in the other extreme, a lifeboat."

Falk's brow furrowed. "Remember, the ship was torn apart and rebuilt into a hotel since she's been in Long Beach. Wherever it's hidden, it's not going to be easy to find."

Koski rolled her tawny-speckled green eyes. "Well, that doesn't necessarily rule out the gym, or any other location that has lots of hiding places for that matter."

Falk's male intuition told him that Metcalf had to choose a never-disturbed, almost inaccessible place; a location where maintenance, cleanup, and refurbishing crews had no reason to set foot. He sighed. Which could admittedly be a gym.

"Okay," he said, "we'll check out the gym and other rooms that offer hiding places, and work our way toward the bow."

"Oh, by the way," Koski reached into a pocket of her jacket

and produced a three-by-five envelope, "Beard gave me this." She opened it and carefully produced a folded sheet of plastic.

Falk wrinkled his brow. "Looks like plastic kitchen wrap."

"Does, doesn't it? But it's a chemical wrap developed by R and D at a lab here in California. It was initially intended for use in high-risk chemical experiments. It's designed to neutralize leakage. We're supposed to immediately wrap it around the briefcase when we find it."

She slid the wrap back into the envelope and replaced it in her pocket. "If we find it."

"We'll find it."

He pulled opened the back door of the bakery shop, which led to a long passageway amidships, and turned to look back at her.

"At the end of this corridor is an elevator. We'll take it down to an area once used for baggage storage. From there we'll take a stairway to a disused, horizontal conduit that runs the length of the ship, stem to stern. We'll follow…"

"Wait," she said. "How large is this conduit?"

Falk drew back with an exaggerated look of appraisal, as if calculating Koski's petite frame in relation to the size of the pipe.

"You'll make it."

She didn't laugh.

"I was thinking more of my…well, trouble with tight places." She shrugged. "Okay. Forget it. I'll survive."

Falk cocked his head and looked down at her. "Sure?"

She glared. "I said I'd be okay."

He gestured toward the long corridor. "We'll follow the

conduit about half the length of the ship, until we're over the number three boiler room, aft of the forward turbo generator room. Then the stairs to R deck and the elevator to the gym."

Koski sighed heavily. "If you could make this any more complicated, you would, right?"

"Koski, we can't just stroll through the damn ship. There's supposed to be no one left aboard. If this guy sees us, he's liable to decide to detonate." He broke off, not wanting to go there. "Look, believe it or not, it's the quickest and maybe the only way to get forward without his seeing us, in the event he's somewhere besides the bow, which he might be."

"It sounds as if you know this ship pretty well."

"Information delivered to me at Van Nuys Airport. I memorized as much as I could during my delay."

As sense of imminent danger ticked at Falk's brain. "Koski, did Heeley say who stabbed Metcalf?"

"He suspects a Panamanian cartel that's using hotels in Panama as fronts for drug running."

Falk did some quick calculations. "Panama is three hours ahead of us, same as the East Coast." He checked his watch. "It's eleven here, so it's two p.m. in Panama. The news of Bonecutter holding the ship hostage was on FOX at eight-thirty this morning, California time; that would be eleven-thirty in Panama. If somebody had access to a private jet or even took a commercial flight out of Panama, they could get to California in ten to twelve hours."

Koski shivered and hugged herself, rubbing her upper arms. "Metcalf's killer could have left Panama as much as two and a half hours ago and be here by, say, seven o'clock tonight, our time." She shook her head. "That's cutting it close. He'd have only an hour. And no way could he get on the ship."

"If someone wants to steal your car badly enough they will, despite the number of auto-theft devices you install, right? Well, a clever person could get aboard and create total havoc here in one hour."

She nodded. "So if we don't find what we're looking for soon, we may acquire some serious competition."

Falk started down the corridor. "Yeah, the operative word being 'serious'."

# Chapter 18

In his soon-to-be-over lifetime, Jack Bonecutter had often quoted Samuel Johnson. "Curiosity is one of the permanent and certain characteristics of a vigorous mind." Bonecutter believed it. It was the result of curiosity, satiated daily by a virtual mountain of books and life experiences, planned and unplanned, lived and relived, that filled the stories he wrote with the ring of truth, the voice of authenticity. It was a blessing; also, a curse.

After several hours on the ladder in the dark shaft, he began to wonder what was happening topside. He tried to stifle his curiosity, but without being aware, he had turned back to face the ladder and moved up several dozen rungs.

Earlier, despite the roar of air in the shaft, his ears had picked up a familiar, heavy, steady thumping—the deep, guttural growl of a Huey. The sound was reminiscent of Bien Hoa. It filled his head, turning him inward to a memory he was powerless to dispel. It flooded every crevice of his brain with that remembered day. A day when three of his buddies had died in a minefield and he, unfortunately, had lived.

They had been doing long-range recon and were walking through a seemingly innocent field when suddenly several nearly simultaneous explosions ripped the air. A piece that might have been the heart of one grunt was hurled through space and splattered onto Bonecutter's chest. A chunk of flesh, some part of another friend, fell at Bonecutter's feet. Another nearby soldier was so disintegrated as to leave no visible physical trace of him on earth.

With shards of shrapnel lodged in his crotch, Bonecutter left Bien Hoa, mentally, long before the Huey that would evacuate him put down in the field. And on the litter that carried him away from the carnage, he was heard singing a rhyme, an inexplicable source of solace.

"Simple Simon met a pie man going to the fair..."

Bonecutter was living proof that those who survived suffered deeply and long. All that remained of his friends were scars in his mind. And the circumstances following his return from that tour of duty had done nothing to alleviate the pain.

It was almost comical now to think that for years after he had returned, he and Marissa had actually tried to pretend that he had not changed. Outwardly, he was unaltered, unless you took into consideration the raised, six-inch slash of pink scar tissue that began where his scrotum once was and continued down his right inner thigh. But inside there was always the lingering sense of inadequacy. Army doctors had explained that the degeneration of his sperm-developing tubules was due to too much body heat; what remained of the testicles being forced to reside in an altered section of his lower abdomen.

"We can't guarantee that surgical rearrangement would produce the desired effect," the doctors had said.

The desired effect was reproduction, of course. Marissa

wanted children. Bonecutter, too, longed to procreate.

"I need whole genitals," he had screamed at the doctors, "with gonads and a sustained erection. And I must have sperm with any distribution of chromosomes whatever, so long as the suckers can swim upstream."

But nothing was produced. Except for a palpable void in his and Marissa's togetherness. For years they continued to make love, but it was like prying passion open. Each time became a main event.

Gradually, he relinquished the need to fill her. They fought bitterly, and the cycle of vicious verbal battles ended last week when she gave their relationship its death blow, the announcement that she was pregnant and wanted a divorce to marry her lover.

Bonecutter's thoughts jumped to the present, and he realized that he had taken the remote from his pocket, that his thumb hovered, quivering over the red detonator button. He shuddered and quickly returned the mechanism to his pocket.

He looked at his lighted watch.

He had been on the ladder for three hours. A muscle in his left calf had tightened into a knot, and he maneuvered a hand down to his leg to massage the cramp away.

He was curious, and wondered each minute what was happening on the ship above him and on the dock below. Certainly, everyone had been evacuated, as his note instructed. He had warned that he would begin the fireworks early if a bomb squad came aboard. Had they conformed to his demands? Or were they out there now, waiting for the chance to pick him off?

He wondered what it would be like on deck now, alone, with no other human footfall echoing through the ship. How would it feel to wander in uninhabited staterooms, or the silent cinema, or the grand ballroom when no music echoed from its brocade ceiling?

What was that?

His head suddenly hit something hard. He released one hand from the ladder and felt the object above him. A board. It was the underside of the trap door beneath the chart table. When had his feet covertly carried him upward to the very top of the shaft he had plunged into earlier?

Well, as long as he was here and because he was curious, he would take a quick look. He touched the pocket of his denim jacket once lightly to remind himself of the courage there, the remote and its small red button he could depress at will if he encountered evidence of betrayal.

Slowly he pushed up the slab of wood and looked around the chart room. It was a small area, with only one window, starboard, facing the bay. If he chose to linger here for several minutes, he would not be seen by a dockside sharpshooter. Good. Then the sudden jangle of a phone. A phone! A phone on the ship was ringing!

He froze.

It was the phone on the bulkhead wall in the wheelhouse, just outside the chart room, not twenty feet from him. Was it possible they knew where he was? But, no, other phones at various, apparently random locations were also ringing, resonating in near unison throughout the otherwise eerily silent ship.

No, they didn't know where he was. They were ringing all phones in hopes he would pick up one, allowing them to pinpoint his location. Or they wanted to speak to him. Either way, he would ignore them.

Looking forward through the open door of the chart room and the panoramic windows above the steering and navigational equipment of the wheelhouse ahead, he had a captain's-eye view of the bow. He watched a gull glide to the deck and perch there, preening itself.

The phones continued to ring, a continuous, stereophonic jangle harsh and persistent. Their ringing was urgent and irritating. And Bonecutter was curious. So what if they pinpointed his location? They wouldn't dare send anyone to search the area. And if they did, they would not find him because he would be back in the shaft, and they would surmise that he had left the bridge.

He stomped past the bulkhead, careful not to let himself be viewed from the dock hundreds of feet below, and stood, staring at the insistent instrument. He reminded himself that he was, after all, in charge and could afford to relax his guard somewhat, enough to see what they had to say. They wouldn't dare kill him. He alone knew where the bombs were. They might, if they had the chance, fire to disable him, but it would be tricky from this distance. Finally, he scooped the phone from its cradle on the wall.

"Jack Bonecutter?" a deliberate, nasal voice asked. Bonecutter was silent, only his nervous breathing transmitted across the line. "Listen, Mr. Bonecutter, this is Colonel J. Manley Beard, United States Army. There is something you need to know. Despite our best efforts to evacuate everyone, you are not alone on the ship."

Not alone. What did he mean? Bonecutter managed to remain silent, a flush beginning in his cheeks.

"We are not to blame. You've got to believe that. We followed your instructions to the letter and evacuated all tourists, hotel guests and ship and security personnel in a timely manner. Moreover, I can assure you that there is no police presence on board at this time. None whatsoever."

Beard paused as if summoning courage. "However, there was a Girl Scout troop on the tour early this morning, and one of the girls, a helpless little child only ten years old, apparently got separated from her troop and is presently unaccounted for."

"It's not true," Bonecutter said harshly. "What kind of gimmick is this?"

"No trick. I swear. She is, I'm told, a precocious child, very inquisitive and bright. And we have reason to believe that she is deliberately hiding on the ship somewhere."

"You must think I'm an idiot!" Bonecutter exploded. "Don't tell me this. I don't want to hear it!"

His head began to ache and throb. He had planned everything so carefully, given them more than ample time to get everyone off the ship so that no one would be hurt.

He shuddered as his spine prickled icily. If they did not find her by eight, she would be killed. No! Oh, God, no! He was not a killer.

He felt pressure building against his temples, the too-familiar shrinking feeling of a spell, but Beard's voice, now seeming to come to him through a long hollow tunnel and carrying unthinkable implications, kept him momentarily in the present.

"Mr. Bonecutter, I'm a soldier. I agonize over every decision I make, especially when human lives are at stake. I've read your war record. You were a brave warrior. My decision to make this call was in the earnest hope that you are reasonable and will agree to let us send a team aboard to search for the girl."

"No!" Bonecutter screamed. "No, Goddammit! I'll find her." He slammed down the phone. He would find her. He had to. He buried his face in his hands. Oh, God. It was supposed to be just the Queen Mary and him.

He set his mouth grimly, turned and headed for the interior stairway leading down to the officers' quarters. He'd start there. He knew the ship like the back of his hand. There wasn't a place on it where one could hide from Jack Bonecutter. He looked at his watch. High noon.

As he left the wheelhouse, the phone made a sorry jingle, as if it suffered a shock, and then died. In the same instant, he felt a shudder from deep in the belly of the vessel; the lights dimmed and flickered, suggesting that somewhere on the ship the electricity was failing.

# Chapter 19

Willie Dill purposely got separated from Girl Scout Troop 892 in the Trafalgar Square Gift Shop during the chaos that followed the order to evacuate the ship. The pre-teen girls, ages eight to eleven, utilized the buddy system, but Willie had sworn her partner to silence. She insisted that she simply must go back to the old projection room adjoining the theater she had glimpsed earlier, where a bank of television monitors maintained surveillance of the ship's interior and exterior, and several computers sitting on a desk had caught her eye.

"But why do you have to go back to that room?" her partner asked.

"Because it's there. Because it's a cool place. Because we're being evacuated and who knows what's going on. Because, well, I'll bet those computers are full of tons of information."

Her friend nodded her agreement, concluding that Wilomena Jean Dill had to uncover the dark secrets that undoubtedly existed on the attendant hard drives.

"Even though the police didn't give a reason for making us leave the ship," Willie's companion argued, "and even though most bomb threats we hear these days turn out to be bogus, there might really be a bomb somewhere." Willie pooh-poohed the idea, but the girl persisted. "Besides, the projection room is way back in the cinema. You might not be able to find your way to the exit."

But Willie's insistence had prevailed, and the girl agreed not to report her buddy missing until the Scout troop got down to the dock and were back on the bus.

While the other scouts were shuffled out of the gift shop, Willie huddled behind a rack of T-shirts in the corner. She was small for her age, and the top of the tiered rack stood a foot above her head.

In her green Girl Scout skirt and a white sweatshirt nearly covered by her green Girl Scout sash, she blended perfectly with the tees on the rack. Patches and pins adorned her sash, including the "Point, Click, Go Try It" award she earned in Brownies.

Her most recent accomplishment was the troop's web site. She had designed it, replete with Scout songs, yellow smiley faces, and recently added a chat room. She had plans for a chat schedule to be up and running soon, so that her troop could talk electronically to girls all over the world.

Willie was in fifth grade, having skipped fourth in the private school she attended. She did not consider herself a nerd. Soon enough, more girlish issues would have to be confronted, even by Willie. Presently, however, other considerations occupied her mind.

For example, when two of her friends' computers recently crashed, they pleaded with Willie to restore them, because their parents said it was too expensive to hire a technician. Both computers, Willie suspected, had simply fallen prey to an internet virus. She told the girls that her own computer was not prone to such trivial nuisances as viruses.

"How come?" they asked.

"I have an on-line e-mail filter that deletes ninety percent of questionable mail, and I keep both a virus program, IPE, and an e-mail bomb catcher running at all times to warn me about any mischievous mail before it ever gets to me," she explained.

"Then, of course," Willie went on unasked, "I have my own modified browser that is not as vulnerable to bombs as others. Moreover, I have a backup system that consists of two hard drives in both of my computers. The second hard drive checks the first and eliminates any intentionally damaging insertions, and every week I use a special backup program to save a full, clean backup."

"Okay," one of her friends interrupted, uninterested in her friend's technobabble. "So can you just come over and fix my computer?"

"Sure," Willie promised, and she planned to do so tomorrow.

When she had ducked behind the T-shirt rack earlier, she pinched her eyes shut behind her thick glasses with their large, dark frames, not wanting to see the moment of discovery if it came. But it didn't.

Soon the shop was silent, clerks having been forced to leave hurriedly with the rest. She stuffed three packages of cheese and crackers and a candy bar into her backpack, left five dollars on the counter, and split, eager to find the old projection room and computers.

She made her way down a long, thickly carpeted corridor. After testing various passageways and doors, Willie Dill, techie genius, had to concede that she was hopelessly lost.

# Chapter 20

Marshak learned of the partial power outage aboard the ship when he returned to Beard's outer office following a trip to the can. He resented the fact that Beard had talked to Bonecutter without letting him know in advance.

*Damn!* And another thing: Beard still had not seen fit to share with him the reason why the military was involved in what Marshak considered a local problem. Not even a reliable rumor stirred as to the military's interest. And Marshak would be damned if he'd ask.

Beard was standing by the computers that were manned by his young communications experts, Miller and Nakamura. Together they awaited the conclusion of a printout, and Marshak deduced from Beard's expression that it was not good news.

Beard ripped it from the printer and sighed, then handed it to Marshak. "What do you think, Captain? Bonecutter's work?"

According to the data, a generator shutdown had caused loss of power to a large portion of the ship, mainly the lower level decks and holds; the PA system and phones in some areas were out.

"The next best thing to knowing the answer to a question,"

Marshak said smugly, "is knowing where to *get* the answer. At my earlier request, the chief engineer has been standing by in the next trailer in case we need him. Looks like we do."

Within minutes the four were standing before a startled engineer. He was a middle-aged man in conservative blue slacks and short-sleeved white shirt with Bob stitched in dark blue thread on the pocket. No doubt his job had been routine and mundane until today, and his uneasy body language said that while engineering might come easy to him, conversation did not.

After considering the specific areas of power failure, Bob said, "As you know, or you may not, umm, portions of the ship have their own power plants, fitted with steam-powered generators. There are several, well, all kinds of built-in safety devices, some computerized, some not, to prevent a generator from exploding."

"Yes, yes." Beard was noticeably impatient.

"Well, it appears that a generator must have registered a fault."

"A fault?"

"So the protective equipment kicked in," the engineer said with a slight "duh" tone in his voice.

Marshak, like Beard, was antsy for the bottom line, but seeking Bob's input being his idea, he was patient. "Yes, go on."

"Errr, I guess I should start from the beginning." Bob's vision flickered to the floor then back up. "You see, if a fault occurs in a generator, or between it and the first circuit breaker, then the generator has to withstand the short-circuit current until its field is automatically switched off by computer. After this short-circuit occurs, automatic equipment disconnects the generator, isolating it from the rest of the system."

He paused to see if they required further explanation, and Marshak, who did not understand at all, looked at Beard. Beard's equally quizzical expression told Bob to go on.

"This reduces the generator's excitation so that the terminal voltage decreases instantly." Another pause. "This shuts down its prime mover and takes the generator completely off-line."

"Look, man, just tell us how this could happen. What caused the fault to begin with?" Marshak asked.

Again the engineer's eyes momentarily sought the floor. "Might be a mis-set. We were told to leave immediately."

Beard cleared his throat. "Since so much of this operation is computerized, can we get the generator started again by computer, from right here?"

"'Fraid not. I can't chance it without going to the site itself and checking out the equipment. It could be as simple as a sticky valve, but it could also be a fault in the feed-water pump."

Beard stopped him by gripping his shoulder and jolting it in the same way he shook hands. "Thank you, Bob. We appreciate your input." He turned the man toward the door and patted him on the back. "We'll let you know if we need you again."

Beard paced his office then eased into his chair. Marshak stood in the doorway. "Why would Bonecutter knock out only one generator?" Marshak wondered aloud.

"Why would he knock out any generator?" Beard asked.

"Colonel, shouldn't we have explored with that engineer the reasons why the backup generator didn't kick in?" Marshak asked.

Beard dismissed the policeman's curiosity with the infuriating vagueness that was getting under Marshak's skin. "Our operatives can figure it out."

*Yeah, right,* Marshak thought: the blonde female agent and the guy flown by chopper to the stern earlier. He also wondered how the two "operatives" would operate this evening, about six, when the clouds that were gathering ushered in the storm and early darkness, and they were still searching frantically for bombs while trying to apprehend a maniac. Well, it was Beard's call.

Earlier Marshak suggested they try to locate Bonecutter's wife, who was on vacation in the West Indies. It was possible, Marshak speculated, that she could talk her old man out of this. Marshak's woman could talk him out of, or into, almost anything.

But Beard had countered, "No need involving some hysterical female. Besides, she's divorcing the guy. Having somebody else's kid, I understand. I doubt there's any love lost between the two at this point."

Marshak wasn't so sure. He'd been married previously, three times, in fact. He figured he probably didn't have the world's biggest heart, but a piece of it still throbbed with some affection for every woman he had ever loved. He shrugged. But this wasn't his operation anymore.

The phone rang. "It's for you, Captain, the Chief on line three."

With a phone to his ear, fielding questions from the Police

Chief, Marshak suddenly thought of the unopened envelope literary agent Pete Powers had left in his office earlier. No doubt it was buried under reports, printouts, and the swimsuit issue of a sports magazine he picked up from the kiosk when he went for cigarettes.

Whatever was in the envelope, which might be an offer for the movie rights to his view of this fiasco, he conjectured, would have to wait a few more minutes. Right now he needed to remain here where the action was.

The little girl on the ship bothered the hell out of him. He had a granddaughter about her age. *Damned kid, gumming up the works*, he cursed mentally, and popped an antacid tablet into his mouth before blatantly lying to his superior on the phone. "Not to worry, Chief. I can say with specificity that we should have this wrapped up by, say, three o'clock, latest."

Miller, on one of the other lines that was insistently ringing, put it on hold and looked up at Marshak. "It's Willie Dill's parents, Nancy and George Dill, on line four, Captain."

"Great!" Marshak thundered and punched the flashing white button.

# Chapter 21

The Bondesque thrill of the chase that was so romanticized, the notion of dashing agents capturing foreign spies passing highly classified secrets in exotic locales—that was mostly fiction, Koski thought. This was what it usually came down to: crawling on hands and knees like a sewer rat through an old pipe in the bowels of a ship, your lung capacity seriously reduced by the close, stagnant air.

It would help if she could see. Just ahead, Falk's body swayed from side to side, alternating hip and knee joints as he made steady headway on all fours.

But no light penetrated the forty-eight-inch, circular conduit they were worming through on their way to the forward section. Koski's open eyes might as well have been closed. There were no grays, no shades of black on black, simply depthless, solid ebony that she felt pushing directly into her, attempting to smother her. *Just keep moving. And don't think about it. That's the key.*

It was at times like this Koski appreciated her prior employment as a videographer for the Nevada Bureau of Land Management. Trained at the FBI Academy at Quantico, she was an excellent markswoman and held a degree in criminal science. Originally she had turned down the FBI, taking the BLM position. It was in that capacity that she had worked with Falk, uncovering a foreign plot to take over the United States from within while pinning it on Native Americans.

Because they had worked so well together, and because she wanted to pair with Falk again, she was here, feeling the walls of the dark conduit close in on her.

A trickle of perspiration ran down her forehead and settled in the corner of her eye. Each breath took its time coming now. "How much farther?" she wheezed.

"Not far." The reply echoed back, muffled but in Falk's usual, optimistic tone.

At this moment she thought it insufferable at the way he always looked at the "bright side." Were they heading out of the conduit or going farther into it? Falk would reply with the most positive response.

He was so different from David, her ex-significant-other. David was a moody, cynical, Reno vice cop who had been busted with cocaine he'd confiscated from a perp when he decided to keep and use it. He was serving time in Susanville prison and Koski seldom thought of him now.

Something else nearly died then: Koski's confidence in her own instincts. She had totally trusted and believed in David. And had been totally wrong.

Working with Falk had helped her regain a portion of her self-confidence, and, with him, she felt she was on the way to full recovery. Not that Falk himself fostered that in her. On the contrary, when they met, he was a loner who obviously resented having a partner.

Yet, while she had proven herself on their previous assignments, some of that nagging self-doubt remained. And what of the emotional tie that she felt slowly developing between them? Both stretched like strings of catgut on an old guitar, ready to twang if properly strummed, yet capable of snapping at any moment.

Koski again became aware of the encircling walls, the stifling, still air, the coal black darkness. She thought she tasted a cool water, like an ice cube in her mouth, and mentally crunched them into wet jewels; the false sensation, however, merely heightened her anxiety.

Then, suddenly, the darkness switched off. Koski saw an orange glow in a recess ahead, revealing Falk in silhouette. When she realized it was a flashlight in his hand, she moaned.

"You mean, you've had a flashlight all along? And here we are, fumbling our way in the dark!"

"Preserving the batteries," he said, his voice resounding off the close curvature of the walls.

"For what?" Koski was working hard just to breathe.

"An emergency."

"Shit! What could be more of an emergency than this?"

"Anything that might unexpectedly come up. Don't talk, Koski. Save your breath."

The light died and Falk crawled on as if unconcerned. He did not want to tell his anxious companion that he thought he had heard water. It occurred to him then that when the ship was fully operational, this conduit would have been automatically flooded in the event of breech, fire or explosion.

Having found no evidence of moisture on the dusty but otherwise nearly clean surface in front or behind, Falk speculated that the automatic safety device that would have likely triggered a flood had been disconnected during the ship's original refitting. Or it was down due to the temporary power failure.

Realistically, he could not discount either "what if." Or others, like, what if the automatic safety device was not disconnected and awaited only a second, confirmatory sensor command to fire? What if one of Bonecutter's bombs was to go off at this minute? Would the explosion trigger the flooding? He envisioned a rush of dark water spiraling toward them. There might be regular intersecting "safety" pipes, and, if so, he would need the light to find it. The pang of unease at the thought started to rise in him, but it quickly passed.

Falk knew himself. It was when a situation seemed most out of his control, that he felt the most confident. At this moment, the challenge was enough to supercharge his capacity to deal with it and he felt a full measure of concentration, inner strength, and—it only happened when he was in high gear like this—a groove. From the day an assignment began until it ended, the rhythm of his life was automatic and harmonious. When fully activated, he was propelled by an instinct that was at once delicate and feral.

Falk's marriage to Meg had been good, but did nothing to help him make order out of this undomesticated aspect of his psyche. Meg. It was nearly five years since she died, but it seemed like yesterday.

A full investigation proved that the stray hunter's bullet found her by accident; there was no one to directly blame, the police report said. Yet there were still days and nights when Falk blamed himself, despite all the therapist's words to the contrary.

It was one of the reasons he had became a loner. One of the reasons he felt out of step with life when an assignment, which kept his mind busy, was over.

Now he had met a woman whose mere presence at a mission's conclusion tended to smooth the transition so that the distinction between feral and domestic blurred without diminishing the strength of either. And he unconsciously vowed in this minute that if they got through this assignment, he'd find the time and the way to tell her.

# Chapter 22

Koski was fighting for air again, and furiously. She thought of only one thing, and it froze like a block of ice in her brain: She could not turn around. If something happened ahead, she would have that long, black eternity to retrace, crawling backwards, because she could not turn around. If something happened behind her, she would have to scramble ahead. To what? How far? No up, no down, no sides. She could not turn around!

Anxiety rose to a panic that heightened the certainty of suffocation. Her heart seemed to swell in her chest. She was about to scream. She had to scream. She had to beat her fists against the walls, to trample Falk, to do anything necessary, anything to get out.

Abruptly the terrifying sensations and compulsions receded, and an exquisite dizziness prickled across her brain, bringing a rush of heat. Now hot water seemed to fill her, bathing her from the inside out, soothing, lulling her away to a black depth that promised a perverse peace. Some small part of her relinquished to it before, finally, from a seemingly vast distance, a voice, Falk's voice, recalled her.

"This is it. This is where we get out." He flashed the light ahead, revealing a side-chamber with four steps built into a steel wall.

Koski lunged forward, crowding him, scrambling up the steps to the freedom of a lower deck, hungrily gulping and gasping for air.

Falk, following, grabbed for her. "You okay?"

She straightened and breathed easier, pulling away. "Of course," she said with obvious irritation. "I'm fine."

Falk watched color return to her pallid cheeks, then bent and brushed off the knees of his pants.

"Classic."

"Pardon?"

"Classic," he repeated, "Panic, a sense of suffocation, near loss of consciousness. All typical of claustrophobia." He straightened and smiled. "But you were a trouper; I'm proud of you."

He knew that she was still shaken, and he was certain that that, more than anything he could do, his words would cause her to pull herself together. One thing he had learned about this woman: When threatened or made to feel vulnerable in any way, she reacted by getting royally pissed off.

She looked dead into his eyes and demanded, "So where are we going now? What are we waiting for?"

He wanted to hug her, but answered simply, "We take the elevator to R deck. It opens to the gym."

They fell silent then, hurrying to the elevator where he punched the "Up" button. There was one other thing he desperately wanted to tell Koski, but would have to wait. Aside from the fact that he preferred to work alone, and despite her claustrophobia, in any life-and-death situation, he felt most comfortable with her, above all people, at his side. They entered the elevator together.

When the elevator eased humming and the doors slid open, they started to move, then froze. Falk's finger went to his lips. Was that which he heard a slight shuffling of feet? Were they lucky, or unlucky, enough to have found Bonecutter already?

Falk slipped the Beretta from its holster seconds before Koski's automatic cleared her waist. Silently they fanned out of the elevator, weapons leveled.

Falk let his vision sweep the room, which was high, long and broad, with gleaming wood floors and windows on both sides. There were several free-weights, treadmills, bikes, stair machines, aerobics gear, a juice bar, and a cardiovascular center, a full line of health and fitness equipment. Falk moved slowly into the room, Koski to his left.

At the far end of the room, near the entrance to the spa, sauna and pool, a punch bag suspended from a beam was swinging, its movement causing an almost imperceptible creak...creak... creak at the juncture of its connection to the chain from which it hung. Otherwise the room was silent. Someone, only moments earlier, had...a flash...a girl bolted from behind the juice bar to their right and raced for the elevator.

"Whoa!" Falk, re-holstering his weapon, swung around and caught her waist as she tried to escape to his right and behind him. "Hold on!" he shouted.

She was a small, wiry bundle of kicking, screaming juvenility.

"Ow," Falk hollered as she sank her teeth into his left wrist, and he released her.

"Wait!" Koski said. "Wait." Returning her 9 mm to its waist holster, she gently but firmly restrained the girl, squatting to make eye-level contact. "Listen. It's okay. We're not going to hurt you, I promise. It's okay."

Reluctantly, the girl stopped wriggling and adjusted her green Girl Scout sash and dark-rimmed glasses. She had a pretty face, with large hazel eyes that were serious and not afraid.

"Everybody was evacuated," the girl said in an irritated voice. "What are you doing here?"

"What are we...?" Falk stuttered.

Koski, rolling her green eyes up at him, their tawny specks flashing, smoothed the girl's sash around her shoulders. "We're police officers, assigned to be sure everyone gets off the ship safely."

She stood but retained one of the girl's hands in a friendly way. "What happened? Did you get separated from the others? Are you lost?"

"I came here on a field trip with Girl Scout Troop 892."

When she offered no further explanation, Koski said, "I see. But they've all left the ship and gone home. How did it happen that you didn't leave with them?"

The girl met Koski's stare proudly. "I hid in the gift shop."

"You hid," Falk said, incredulous. He thrust his hands into the air and turned away in frustration, then moved toward the windows on the bay side of the ship.

"You didn't want to leave?" Koski asked the girl.

She shook her head from side to side but remained silent.

Koski sighed and led her to a nearby bench. "What's your name?"

"Wilomena Jean Dill. People call me Willie."

Koski offered her hand. "Pleased to meet you, Willie. What a nice name. I'm Susan Koski. That's my partner, Joe Falk, over there. How old are you, Willie?"

"Ten. I'm in the sixth grade. I skipped fourth."

Falk had heard all he needed to hear. He pressed gently on his phone ear-bud. "Colonel, Agent Koski and I are in the ship's gymnasium, where we've encountered a ten-year-old Girl Scout named Wilomena Jean Dill. Was there something you forgot to tell me?"

Beard's harsh, nasal voice answered. "Ah, yes, I was just about to call you about her. Good, I'm glad you found her." Beard paused as if attempting to figure out what he should say next. "I wish I could get word to Bonecutter that we have her in custody, so to speak; might ease the trigger finger on that remote of his."

"You wish what, sir?"

"Ah, yes. Well, you see, he has no means of communication, and the damned phones and PA system on the ship are temporarily out, as is electrical power in certain portions of the vessel. We don't know yet what caused the outage, but we're told that it could be a generator in the amidships boiler room."

Falk gnashed his teeth. He was about to say that the ship's

generators were not exactly his responsibility when Beard went on.

"We need that generator on line, agent Falk. It controls our video lifeline to the interior and exterior of the ship. We need it to maintain full surveillance capabilities." His voice tapered off.

"I have some general knowledge of generators," Falk said, "but I'm no engineer." He looked at his watch; it was past noon. "And we need to find…"

He glanced toward Koski and the girl and knew by the way Koski ignored him that she was paying close attention, probably hoping he would not say anything that might scare the girl.

He lowered his voice and moved farther away.

"Time is running out for us to carry out our primary assignment, sir."

"Yes, yes, of course." Beard paused on his end of the line.

Falk took a deep breath and listened while Beard conveyed the essential information regarding the generator and boiler room. "Okay, I know where that boiler room is located. I'll take a quick look."

"Good man. When you return to the gym, call us. We'll have a plan worked out to get the girl off the ship."

Falk knew that the chances of Bonecutter, wherever he was, learning that Falk and his partner were on the ship were increasing with every passing minute. And the crazy bastard had made it crystal clear in his note that he would detonate his bombs sooner than eight o'clock if his instructions were not precisely followed. Falk ended the conversation with the colonel.

"Look," he said to Koski, rejoining them, "I've got to check out one of the generators. It'll take a few minutes, maybe ten. It might not hurt for you to scope the gym for the...for my briefcase, which I foolishly forgot when we were here earlier." He pointed a finger at the girl. "You can help us by..."

"Oh good!" The youngster was instantly on her feet. It seemed that her resentment at their intrusion into her plans had passed and now she was ready to play detective.

Falk put a hand on each of her shoulders and gently pressed her back down to the bench. "I understand that it's part of the Scout promise to help people at all times. You can help us by staying here with Koski for a few minutes, right where you are. That means you don't move from that spot until I get back, understand? Promise?"

He gave Koski what he hoped was an optimistic look, but as he turned and hurried to the elevator, a prickle of frustration danced through his nervous system. For the first time since he started this assignment he had some doubts as to its successful conclusion.

# Chapter 23

When his second meeting with Daystar executives concluded at noon, CEO Lew Blasingdon had heard no suggestions for exploitation of the Queen Mary situation better than his own, which he declined to divulge. This, then, would be his show, and his alone.

Blasingdon learned long ago that the reputation of power is what ultimately gave one power, and he had both in abundance. But power bred isolation, and isolation slowly broke down the channels of communication he once relied on to create his reputation.

More and more, he had to keep strategic corporate information to himself, and this made him less apt to rely on the judgment of others who, he naturally concluded, lacked facts. This, his wife said, made him capricious. Perhaps that was so, for he was about to commit the most capricious act of his life.

He phoned his pilot, telling him to be at the helipad atop the Daystar tower and ready to fly to Long Beach. Now. Sooner, if possible.

The intercom buzzed, interrupting his mental selection of the best remote camera operator for the job. Pete Powers here to see him about Bonecutter, it advised. Blasingdon recalled that Powers was considered a first-rate cameraman before he turned agent. It wasn't as if the shots he wanted had to have cinematic excellence; Computer Graphics Division and Post could fix up almost anything. The important thing was to get something live.

Less than two hours later, Powers was cramped in the silver chopper to the side of Dan Hansen, the pilot, and Blasingdon. The CEO didn't care about Powers beyond his camera skills. In fact, the man looked sick. He'd gone to Blasingdon to persuade him to call Marshak, to bring Daystar's clout to bear on the uncooperative police captain.

Blasingdon had smiled benevolently. "I'll do better than that, Pete. I'm going to Long Beach to talk to this Marshak asshole in person." As if it were a gift, he added, "And I'm taking you with me."

Powers had thanked Blasingdon for the response, especially since his and Chaum's earlier attempt had failed. It wasn't until they were in the helicopter that Powers learned what his role was to be. Blasingdon would not approach Marshak until he'd obtained enough on-the-spot footage to pre-sell "Death of the Queen Mary," Blasingdon's working title for the upcoming big-screen version of today's events. If Bonecutter lived to pull off the bombing, Blasingdon's minions, who were now racing down the Harbor freeway toward Long Beach to be there for the eight o'clock main event, would capture it from a dock's eye view.

If the explosions were as spectacular as Blasingdon hoped, mountains of film would be ready for "Death of the Queen

Mary," and what was not immediately used would swell the vaults of Daystar's stock footage library. The scenes Powers was about to film would add a sense of richness and the personal touch that Blasingdon so coveted and sometimes managed, in his impersonal way, to attain.

As they approached San Pedro, Blasingdon tapped Powers, who he saw was still trying to make sense of innovations in remotes since the last one he had operated.

"Listen, Powers," Blasingdon said, his usually soft voice sounding loud and brayish, "get me some good footage, and your entire stable of writers will be working for a long, long time."

# Chapter 24

Pete Powers fiddled with the camera, examining its menu of shooting modes. Ordinarily, he would have salivated at the prospect of Blasingdon throwing work his way. But he lived by his hunches, and, years ago, when he read Jack Bonecutter's first script, he had a hunch that here was someone who could make an agent proud, and substantially rich. Well beyond that, he felt as though he had found a friend in Jack, and he was right.

His mind suddenly formed a black silhouette of the Queen Mary inside a red circle with a red slash through it: NO FILMING, his intuition warned. Instead, they must get the hell out of there. Yet, his compunction to help Jack plus the power of Blasingdon's offer edged out his inner voice.

He turned back to Blasingdon and shouted, "Don't forget. The deal is, I get you some live footage, and you'll get us on the ship afterwards to talk to Jack, right?"

The mogul gripped Pete's shoulder from behind. "You have my word on it."

Pete steadied the camera against the side of his face as he caught sight of the magnificent ocean liner in the distance. Could Blasingdon be trusted? In a far corner of his mind, he heard Sam Goldwyn say, "In two words: im-possible."

Leaning close to the pilot's ear, Blasingdon shouted, "When we get there, take her in low, Hansen. Let's begin by going along the length of the ship, a couple of times on each side."

Powers could see that Hansen was edgy. They were informed at take-off that no aircraft were allowed near the ship. How far were the authorities prepared to go to keep air space clear since September 11, 2001? Also, the chopper was already fighting some vicious crosscurrents due to the storm that had stalled off shore, but was now moving in.

"I don't know, Mr. B.," Hansen said haltingly. "There's a strong wind out there. Dock side may be okay, but it could be dangerous on the weather side."

"Don't worry about the weather," Blasingdon shouted, as if it, too, were under his control. "We'll only be here a few minutes." He rephrased his earlier order more firmly. "Stem to stern, port and starboard, Hansen. I want it all. That's what you get the big bucks for."

# Chapter 25

Falk left the gym and hurried back through the long conduit through which he and Koski had crawled earlier, to the amidship boiler room. Fortunately, rewiring an obviously malfunctioning switch in a glorified fuse box was all it took. The backup generator immediately hummed to life, the tick of his watch on Falk's wrist reminding him that the side trip had cost valuable time from his main mission.

When the elevator to the gym ground to a halt and the door opened, he saw Koski and Willie seated on the bench, chatting, even laughing. He marveled at their casual manner, as if they had always known each other, as if their world was not hours from potential destruction.

Willie seemed particularly at ease. When Koski abandoned her sometimes hard-shelled exterior, she had that effect on others.

"You mean that you, yourself, have actually crashed your own computers?" Koski was asking. She shot Falk a glance as he advanced, and he gave her a thumbs-up to signal he had successfully accomplished his side-mission.

Continuing the charade, she opened her arms in the empty

gesture that told him she had searched the gym and found neither briefcase, explosive charge nor Bonecutter.

Willie wiggled her nose to readjust her large glasses, and then pushed a chubby finger at them just above the bridge of her nose. Her expression was luminous.

"Oh, yes, I crash them once or twice a year, trying new hardware or attempting to customize new programs to my needs." She smiled, and her hazel eyes brimmed with amusement. "My mom and dad say that I'm much more dangerous than any computer virus."

Falk flipped open his cell phone as he walked up to them.

"Hi, Joe," Willie said, as if they were old friends.

Falk nodded. "I'll call Beard," he told Koski, "and we'll get our little Brownie here to safety."

"Brownie!" Willie protested. "I got my wings a long time ago. I'm a second-year junior."

Falk was about to communicate with Beard when he glanced toward the window facing the bay and saw a helicopter heading straight toward the ship. He stumbled across the gymnasium, his vision focused on the silver aircraft that was ignoring the air space restriction around the Queen Mary. The sight of it, nosing directly at them, so mesmerized him that he was hardly aware that Koski and the girl had come up behind him.

The chopper dipped and swayed against a strong westerly wind and came in loud, low, and fast, three men clearly visible behind the glass bubble of its cockpit. In that moment, the din of its motor reached a deafening pitch and it seemed the machine would burst through the window where Falk stood riveted. The pilot made a last-minute lateral maneuver, sweeping the craft up and to the right, out of sight, the clatter of its rotors veering with it.

Koski articulated Falk's thought. "Who are those idiots?"

# Chapter 26

Bonecutter was separated from the gymnasium by one deck and the second of the three funnels as he continued his search for the Girl Scout. He entered a room originally called The Cinema Box, the room that projected movies through the famous unicorn carving into the amidship ballroom. He thought how once a projectionist, ancestor of today's video jockeys, had spun his magic here with clumsy, clattering reels of film, unraveling moving pictures that were now being digitally restored for late-night television.

Crossing the room, he examined a bank of functioning television monitors along one wall. They were running on backup batteries. Like hazy photographs, they displayed interior and exterior images of the ship, in color, but with less than up-to-the-minute clarity. He eased into one of the chairs and surveyed the layout. Had he discovered a means of scanning the ship without leaving this room?

He'd spent enough time in projection rooms, watched enough movie and television dailies to have a working knowledge of a console. Slowly he moved a slide switch and the pictures dimmed. Returning the switch to its original position caused the images to come up to near-normal brightness. He turned a large, notched knob, and filled the room with the screech of feedback before he quickly reversed it. So now he knew where the master volume control was.

One by one, he gingerly tested the controls, ten remote cameras in all, each operated from the console where he sat. He was euphoric. If he could observe large portions of the ship from this closed-circuit television system, then sooner or later, the girl likely would show up on one of the monitors. And then he could get the little pain in the ass off the ship.

He was about to shift his glance from the clear, amidships shot that he supposed was being furnished by an exterior camera high in the superstructure, when he saw the silver helicopter come into view. He gasped. He knew that aircraft. Hadn't he and his wife Marissa once flown on one like it? At once he wondered where Marissa was, unable as we was to remember why she wasn't here with him. With the greatest effort, he forced himself to concentrate back on the console.

Clumsily at first, then quickly getting the feel, his fingers manipulated the camera control, tracking the helicopter. He followed the erratic, weaving machine, aware of the pilot's difficulty controlling it in the high wind as he repeatedly buzzed the ship.

Fingering the zoom lens control, Bonecutter was able to zero in on the picture, closer and closer, until he could see the familiar face of Lew Blasingdon peering out through the expanse of glass. Blue letters emblazoned on the chopper announced Daystar Studios. Then Bonecutter recognized the nervous pilot. And seated beside him, trying to maneuver a remote camera was Pete Powers.

"What the fuck?"

Bonecutter watched in disbelief as the aircraft yet again swept the area, swung into a tight turn as if to attempt another run, then vanished from one monitor and entered another. It made its way along the opposite side of the ship, the wind nearly tossing it when it cleared the bow. Trying to give Powers a pick-up shot, Bonecutter figured. He slammed his fist down on the console. "Crazy sons-a-bitches. You're gonna kill yourselves!"

# Chapter 27

When they made their first swing down the side of the ship, Powers' camera did not find the one male and two female faces peering out of the gymnasium window. On the second pass, however, it caught them and might have preserved their surprise for "Death of the Queen Mary" and posterity.

"Wait!" Powers shouted when his camera's unblinking eye saw a blur of the trio behind the window.

"Wait?" Hanson screeched. "Wait? What the hell are you talking about?" He was fighting an updraft that had caught them when he tried to nudge closer to the side of the ship.

While Powers shouted what he'd seen to Blasingdon, Hansen ignored them, and, skillfully avoiding cables and fore-rigging, swooped back over the three majestic smokestacks, and down the weather side of the liner.

Suddenly the cockpit was filled with harsh static, and a voice barely loud enough to overpower it announced, "This is Army Patrol, Skymaster three. You are violating restricted air space. Climb to two thousand feet immediately and identify."

The three men whipped their heads to the right as—WHAAH —the Skymaster helicopter burst into their vision then thundered by.

"Holy shit!" Hansen said. "The Army." The chopper hadn't shown up on his instrument screen. "It must have come up straight from the pier. It has armed waist gunners. After two tours in Nam and one in the Gulf, I'm not going to be shot down in California by my own countrymen."

"Powers," Blasingdon barked as if he had not heard the Skymaster's order, "be sure you get a good shot of those bozos when that chopper comes by again. They're our tax dollars at work, trying to prevent three working stiffs from doing their job."

Pete couldn't believe what he was hearing from Blasingdon, but there was no time to consider. The military was calling the shots; the plot had just significantly thickened.

"The Army thinks we're terrorists, Hansen!" Pete shouted over his shoulder. "Get us the fuck outta here! NOW!"

But Blasingdon was poking the pilot, probably having seen the twitch that said Hansen was about to obey Pete's order.

"Hansen," the CEO said, "don't let these assholes scare you. The military's involvement only means that Bonecutter is now writing the most important story of his life." He leaned closer. "There's a twenty-thousand-dollar bonus, payable in cash on our return to the studio, if you ignore that restricted horseshit a few minutes longer and let Powers get a little more footage. What do you say?"

Hansen was silent as he fought the stick for control against the winds buffeting the craft. Pete could sense the pilot considering Blasingdon's proposition, calculating how risky one more pass might be. They could insist that their radio was out, that they didn't hear and were not aware of the order. Hansen could use the money; he had a wife and kids.

"What the fuck are you doing, Hansen?" Pete shouted. "You're not going to let the prospect of twenty thou' and that ready-when-you-are-C.B. routine make you do something we'll all regret, are you?"

Powers knew that money could cloud a man's thinking, make him lose sight of the difference between need and greed. "Look, I want outta' here right now! You'd better…"

He didn't get a chance to finish, to warn the distracted pilot that the mere act of considering might cause him to misjudge the ferocity of air turbulence that waited for a chance to thrash them. Hansen hesitated one second too long.

The small craft fluttered as a violent gust of wind rocked across its airframe.

Pete's camera fell to his lap. His fingers were a vise on the hand supports as he felt the helicopter writhe to one side, his main concern no longer the camera's eye. Behind him, Blasingdon made a wheezing sound.

Too late, the reflexes rooted in the grooves of his mind that impelled Hansen to try a corrective maneuver cut in. The engine revved as he asked it for power, but the cockpit bounced out of kilter, its weight shifted, and the chopper attempted to lift away, but instead stuttered and froze.

# Chapter 28

What happened next tingled Bonecutter's nervous system array. He felt as if he was there, in the cockpit with his friend and the other two men rather than simply viewing them on the monitor in the old projection room. It felt as if his body was there, suspended along with them as the chopper hung in mid-air for that eternal second. He saw the aircraft dip and do a crazy quarter-turn. Like a swimming fish, it swayed from side to side until the motion grew as violent as a fighting marlin thrashing its tail. Then the tip of the tail rotor assembly made a kiss of contact with the mainmast cable of the Queen Mary.

Careening out of control, the aircraft narrowly missed the upper decks, dropped and slid down the steel side of the ship, leaving a streak of blazing gasoline along the hull. The chopper erupted into a dazzling ball of orange light as its fuel tank exploded an instant before it met water. Flames and chunky metal shot from the aircraft. What little remained of it and its occupants sizzled into the bay.

Bonecutter could remember the scene in split-second images. Pete Powers' lips moved silently, then opened wide in a silent scream. Blasingdon clawed for support, desperate for some alteration of fate. Hansen's fiercely straining grip on the throttle was still trying to make right what would be forever wrong.

Emotion paralyzed Bonecutter. He was shocked, sickened, sad and angry, though surprise was the overriding sensation. Surprise that, at this terminal point in his life, he could still experience other emotions.

Bonecutter's nature was to mourn life's conclusions as the death of dreams. He hardly knew the doomed pilot, but the man must have had hopes and aspirations. Blasingdon, certainly, had his. In fact, his were grandiose, probably too much so and responsible for the deaths of all three men's dreams.

Pete Powers. There was a dreamer, and not only for himself. He had a wife and six kids. And now Pete's dreams for his family and theirs for him were dead.

This last realization draped itself heavily over Bonecutter, and his resolve to die heightened. There were no fantasies that would die with him. And now, more than ever, no one's dreams were contingent upon him. He laughed a little twisted laugh. On one monitor he noticed the debris from the helicopter, bobbing on the water's surface amid a slick of black oil.

He tried to swallow the lump that was constricting his throat. Pete Powers' friendship was Bonecutter's last worthy connection to the world and tonight Pete was already asleep in the sea.

# Chapter 29

Someone thrust a hand mike at Marshak's face.

"It's being reported that the Army shot down the civilian helicopter in which three people died. Is that true, Captain?"

*It's about to be reported that Captain Marshak delivered a neat, sound karate chop to the side of a reporter's head,* Marshak silently said. It bothered him enough that the chopper had crashed, and that Powers, the gutsy guy he now wished he had granted access to the ship, was dead, along with two others.

But now the media hyenas had started doing what they did best, and what Marshak felt was ruining this country: making the news fit their own definition of the public's thirst. Pushing it, squeezing it, bearing down upon it, until fresh news—their interpretation, that is—was born.

He shoved the phallic-looking instrument away from his mouth and growled, "That is not true."

He had left his office minutes earlier to make another of his frequent visits to the john, and been accosted on his return by a dozen members of the press. Somehow they'd gained entrance to the hallway of the command post, where they now surrounded him, pushing in tight, screeching like a cave of startled bats.

Where was security? *If one of these, just one of them gets on that ship...*he dodged another microphone. Damn! Somebody's ass was going to burn for this.

"But, Captain, what's a military aircraft doing patrolling the air space above the Queen Mary?" a young woman, a clone of all the others, persisted. "Do you still maintain that this is not a terrorist attack?"

"This is not a terrorist attack!"

"Have you located the bomber yet?"

Marshak brushed them aside. "No comment." But, like water in a muddy stream, others immediately displaced them.

Someone else's voice managed to isolate itself from the rest. "Will you be holding a media briefing soon?"

Marshak saw a handful of his officers coming to the rescue from the other end of the hall, but he couldn't wait. Elbowing the overzealous men and women from his path, he ground his size fourteens down on toes and propelled his weight against the sea of bodies.

As he reached the door to his office, he turned and, in as controlled a voice as possible, said, "This is a domestic bomb threat, not a world war. When the Chief thinks a media briefing is appropriate, we'll let you know. In the meantime, I suggest you all go home and take cold showers."

Marshak was not a media darling.

Slamming the door behind him, he swore, picked up the phone, and punched at a number. "Get Sergeant Wilson in here, now!" Somebody's ass was going to burn for this.

To be honest, Marshak knew what his problem with reporters

was: patience. He had none. He never saw fit to cultivate it. Not with the fourth estate or anyone else. Giving in to the basic premise of patience went against his grain.

Oh, he knew about patience being rewarded with delayed gratification, about taking one day at a time. All of those were, in his view, pseudo-psychologies. When you got to the bottom line, patience was not a virtue, but a subtle, insidious disease, an atom-sized form of desperation masquerading as high-mindedness. He'd have nothing to do with it.

He lit a cigarette and took one long drag, then placed it in the small, shallow, aluminum foil faux ashtray he'd lifted from the restroom. He began rummaging through the clutter on his desk for the one thing that gnawed at the back of his mind now, the unopened envelope Pete Powers had left for him. Before he could locate it, his intercom sounded, and he was summoned to Beard's office to "go over what we have."

A young Army lieutenant sitting beside Beard's desk rose as the colonel introduced him.

"Captain Marshak, this is Lieutenant Smothers, one of our top-notch PR men." Marshak shook Smothers' hand and took a seat. Beard sighed almost imperceptibly. "Captain, how did the reporters get into Com-Cen?"

Ordinarily, Marshak was cool on the defensive, but it was not his favorite position, especially in front of a green lieutenant. "I was about to investigate that when you invited me in here, Colonel. Sergeant Wilson should be on his way to my office as we speak."

"We agreed to use your personnel, for the most part, in order to attempt to maintain a low profile. However, maybe it's time to call in..."

Marshak stopped him with a palm up. That was all they needed, more bodies to keep track of. "Since the chopper accident, and our subsequent need to investigate it, nothing is low profile anymore, Colonel. We've got boats out in the bay collecting debris and pieces of dead bodies and the NTSB people are flying in. There's no way this situation will ever be low profile again." He paused and straightened. "However, insofar as my responsibility extends, everything is now under control."

Beard pointed to the small portable TV set on his desk. "You were on the news a few minutes ago, Captain. Live and in living color."

Marshak chose to find no racist intent in the last part of that remark, a prerogative he thought underused.

"Pond scum," he said, feeling inclined to air views on the media he generally kept to himself. "Generally," he went on, "people all over the world are getting fed up with the media's intrusive tactics, particularly those of the broadcast media." He shook his head. "At least some of the public is finally starting to put faces on the term 'the media', which the journalistic community uses as if speaking of someone other than itself."

He stopped, suddenly doubting that Beard and the green lieutenant were on the same page as he on this subject.

Beard set his pencil down and leaned back in the chair, his usual clipped, nasal voice taking on a rambling, philosophical tone.

"We once read about a small bird down in Africa that spends its entire life perched on the back of a rhino or hippo. We don't recall which. You would think this would drive the animal mad, but he agreeably abides the pest. As we understand it, the bird survives by pecking away at minuscule creatures, vermin which, in turn, feed on the larger animal's flesh. The bird is also sensitive to its host's predators, apparently, and squawks to warn him of danger."

Marshak, himself a fan of the Discovery, National Geographic channels and Wild Kingdom reruns, sat quietly, containing his impatience. Beard went on, turning at times to include Smothers for affirmation, which the lieutenant provided with short, brisk nods of his head.

"We see the media as the bird," Beard said, "and the rest of the population as the rhino. Or hippo, whichever. They drive us mad sometimes with their pecking and scratching and squawking, but they have their usefulness; they, too, are a part of the big picture, of the system, and maybe we should be more understanding of them."

Marshak, rankled, listened to what he considered to be an outdated, condescending lecture, then answered. "Nevertheless, when the bird takes a dump on his back, the rhino—or hippo—doesn't have to like it or can't be wholly blamed if, after an endless number of pecks and dumps that begin to fester into a sore, he decides to eat the little bastard."

Smothers looked as if all of this went over his head, while Beard cleared his throat and sank his gaze into the papers on his desk. "The helicopter crash was dreadful. Highly unfortunate.

And we will downplay it as much as possible."

The compassionate Marlin Perkins demeanor was gone, Marshak noted. We're all business, now. Beard gestured toward his young companion.

"We've assigned Lieutenant Smothers to handle all future news releases. We, Captain—you and I—will hereafter be *persona non grata* as news sources. Smothers will feed the media the positive stuff: The ship was evacuated without incident. Thanks to the efficiency of the Long Beach Police Department and the security skills of the Queen Mary's personnel, a potential disaster infinitely worse than the helicopter accident will be averted. We have been in communication with Bonecutter and are making every effort to negotiate with him. That sort of thing."

He turned to Smothers for confirmation and was rewarded with, "Understood, sir."

Beard turned back to Marshak. "Did you have anything further to suggest to Lieutenant Smothers, Captain?"

He had a suggestion, all right, but decided it would better keep. He did, however, need some questions answered.

"Since the press has decided to feed the rumor that the Army shot down the studio chopper, it might help clear things up if we told them exactly what the Army is doing here, some hint as to why the military gives a damn about this whole affair."

"Smothers has orders on that." Beard turned to the young man again. "Correct?"

Smothers nodded, stating, "Correct, sir," then directed the rest of his reply to Marshak. "A certain amount of federal involvement is standard procedure where bombs are concerned, especially since 9/ll. Also, several foreign countries have recently been in negotiations with the Queen Mary's owners regarding possible acquisition of the ship.

"Because Mr. Bonecutter's threat could put such possible acquisition in jeopardy, these countries have requested that the military oversee this situation, thereby precipitating the army's presence. Their role, however, is merely an advisory one at this juncture."

He stopped and it was his turn to look to Beard for confirmation that he had correctly presented the rhetoric.

Before Marshak could blow holes in their spin, Beard thanked the lieutenant and dismissed him.

"Now then, Captain," Beard said calmly, leaning back in his chair, "recapping the situation on the ship: We have Bonecutter, two FBI operatives, Falk and Koski, and the Girl Scout, right?"

"Right."

Beard leaned forward again and reached into an In basket on the desk. "In point of fact, there will be one more person arriving this afternoon who, if this situation is not resolved, we'll be obliged to maneuver onto the ship."

"What?" Marshak sprang from his chair. "Man, I don't fucking believe it!"

Beard didn't seem that surprised at the protest, as if he shared Marshak's opinion, but he simply went on. "An agent with British Intelligence is already here in the States, I understand. You see, the Brits have a stake in this."

"It's beginning to look like everybody and his fucking brother has a stake in it, but that doesn't mean…"

"Captain," Beard said, stopping him with a palm up. He slipped the note into the Out basket with its predecessors and eased back again. "What I'm about to tell you can never leave this office. Understood?"

Marshak sighed quizzically and sat down. "Understood."

Beard picked up and fingered his pencil. "I guess it's time I filled you in as to what's really happening on board the Queen Mary."

# Chapter 30

When the aircraft exploded in full view of Falk and his two companions, Koski's protective instinct caused her to grab Willie and fiercely bury the girl's face against her chest, away from the sight, but not before the girl saw much of the disaster. Several minutes of intense consolation followed. She masterfully handled a reassuring talk with Willie.

What signaled the initial stages of disaster syndrome—dazed disbelief, distraction, numbness—was already progressing naturally as Koski soothingly repeated the girl's feelings about what she had witnessed. If indeed any of them lived to get off the damned ship, Falk would recommend that both Willie and Koski talk to a therapist to assimilate the whole shipboard experience. But now, he had to go.

"Koski, call Beard and tell him that we've got Willie and that she's safe, and that you and she are leaving the ship." He adjusted his stance determinedly, setting his feet firmly apart. "I've got to find Bonecutter." He turned and started to move away as if his mere pronouncement had settled the matter.

"Hey!"

Koski was on her feet, in his face. She glowered, then turned back to Willie, whose face mirrored her disappointment at what Falk had planned for her. "Stay there a minute, sweetheart. I need to talk to Falk for a second."

She took his arm and led him back toward the windows, where fire and rescue crews were at work with the wreckage in the bay.

"I'm not leaving this ship, Joe," she whispered firmly.

Falk looked into her resolute eyes, faceted with fiery light.

"Koski, there isn't time to talk about this." He glanced at his watch. "It's almost one o'clock. I don't have…"

"All the more reason why you need an extra pair of eyes and hands, and you know it."

He glared. "Okay, then, stay on the ship. Both of you. But you're on your own. She's your responsibility now. *You* can have yet another pair of eyes. I don't need or want them."

He knew as soon as he said it that it was insane. It would be worse than criminal to deliberately leave the two alone.

Koski turned toward the bench, and paled, but Falk did not need to follow her gaze to know why. He knew, with the sickening intensity of a rock hitting bottom in his belly, that Willie was gone.

# Chapter 31

Marshak still didn't like the idea. There was a briefcase on board with chemical properties so lethal that the very disclosure of its existence would cause irreparable damage to the United States and Great Britain. It didn't change the fact that Marshak was against putting another person on the ship. And what about Beard's two so-called 'operatives', agents Falk and Koski? What were those two hotshots doing?

He headed for the outer office. His day was complicated enough. Minutes before the helicopter crash, as Miller and Nakamura, Com-Cen's communications officers, manned the bank of electronic equipment, Miller had turned to Marshak, his cheeks red with sudden excitement.

"Captain, look. I think…yes. We've got visual back."

Beside him, Nakamura hollered, "Yahoo!"

Marshak turned to the equipment that had been little more than static since the generator had shut down and power and phones failed in select areas of the ship.

"The backup generator has finally kicked in?"

"Affirmative, sir. We're visually hooked into the entire ship again." His elation dimmed as he continued to fiddle with knobs and switches. "However, audio's still out. The PA and phones, too; I don't understand it. The phones should be operational. It doesn't make sense."

Nakamura, nevertheless, was elated. "At least we've got a picture."

Marshak had leaned between the two, so close he could feel the blink of Nakamura's eyelids.

"Never mind pumping your 'nads, Nakamura. Just get the fucking phones working." He straightened. This was a lucky break. Or was it luck? "Who could have restarted the backup generator?" he wondered aloud.

From behind his right shoulder came the level, nasal reply that signaled Beard's entrance. "One of our operatives, of course."

Marshak had no comment. He had to abide the little pests who lived on his back and pecked away at him. Now the phone rang.

Miller picked it up.

"Yes, he's right here," he said and handed the phone to Marshak. "Security at the main gate," he explained.

"What now?" Marshak growled.

"I've got a Mr. and Mrs. George Dill here, Captain," the guard reported. "They say you told them to come."

Marshak swore. "No, I did not tell them to come."

What he had said to Willie Dill's parents, in fact, was that they should stay by the phone at home, and he would contact them as soon as he had any word about their daughter. He sighed. He, himself, was a parent to five grown children. Were it his kid, he wouldn't have stayed at home; he'd want to be as close to the scene as possible.

"Send them to the office adjoining mine," he grumbled. "I'll talk to them there."

As he walked toward the office, he looked out of the window and glimpsed the Dills, hurrying toward his mobile command post. In their forties, they looked like most mothers and fathers looked when their child was in jeopardy: heartsick, bewildered, filled with foreboding. On an ascending scale of one to ten concerning what Marshak hated most about his job, dealing with distraught parents was right up there.

# Chapter 32

In the subsequent hours, Falk and Koski threw every skill they possessed into their search for Bonecutter, his bombs, the briefcase and Willie. Leaving the gym, they first scoured the amidships portion of the vessel, ever cautious, always hoping that they would spot the saboteur before he spotted them.

Falk sweated every corner he turned. Like a triple black diamond ski slope, unmarked obstacles were everywhere. But Falk's mind was focused; he was in his groove, heading forward in optimal drive.

In late afternoon, they found themselves in a galley and reluctantly gave in to hunger, halting long enough to devour slices of turkey from the refrigerator and some fruit.

Falk was tormented by the fact that they had let Willie get away, a misstep both he and Koski would regret all of their lives if they did not find her.

# Chapter 33

"It's him!" Miller's voice cracked, as if articulation of what he saw on the monitor would make it vanish. "It's him," he repeated, softer. "We've got him."

Marshak and Beard rushed to the console.

Pointing to the monitor, Miller adjusted the image and whispered, "I discovered a feed that must have been deactivated at the time of the evacuation, but I've got it back online now. It's a hidden security camera in the projection room of the old theater. And there he is."

The four men stared at the figure seated before the monitors in the ship's projection room.

"It's Bonecutter, all right." Marshak, too, found himself whispering.

It seemed appropriate that the camera allowed them to secretly observe the man. Marshak whipped a large, white handkerchief from his hip pocket and wiped it across his forehead. Bonecutter looked to him to be in a trance, as if he'd been sitting in that exact position for some time.

Beard put a hand on Nakamura's shoulder. "Good work."

On the screen, the man's head nodded forward and then came

up and back, until his distorted face paralleled the ceiling. His eyes were feral and his jaw slack and distended; his mouth cavernous.

It hit Marshak that the poor bastard had probably watched his buddies die in the chopper crash hours before. Maybe he was only now having a reaction to that horrifying event. Or maybe it was something else, something no one could guess, that tortured the man.

Miller's little finger automatically whirled up the audio knob, forgetting it was out of commission. Had they been able to hear the sound, it would have hurtled through the command post, the force of its report strong enough to make them shudder.

Begun like a growl, the sound rose to a piercing, orgiastic howl that held interminably. Then, in cracked and with collapsing notes, it fell to a pitiful whimper, then to a second of utter silence. Then Bonecutter straightened and, in a voice unheard by anyone else, cooed, "Flea, flea, let me be, bloodthirsty busy, busy bee flea."

Bonecutter jumped up and stumbled from the room.

# Chapter 34

There was something in the way the man calmly strode into the command post that instantly decided Marshak. He did not like Simon Drummond. In their little chat earlier about what was behind British Intelligence involvement with the Queen Mary, Beard had told Marshak more than he cared to know about the man from MI6.

"He was hand-picked by the Prime Minister himself," Beard said. "Not only because he happened to be in the States, but because his experience and credentials are impeccable."

Marshak nodded. He'd not lived under a rock for the past fifty years. He had seen the James Bond movies, read some novels in the genre, and he knew all about The Firm.

"Drummond joined British Intelligence after taking his degree at St. John's," Beard went on, "and was called in on the terrorist scare with the QE2. Apparently, he became familiar with every oceangoing vessel exceeding one thousand tons, which includes the Queen Mary, of course, speculating that any one of such ships might one day be the target of a terrorist attack. Such conscientious investigation included keeping abreast of configuration changes in this ship since she was acquired by your city, Captain."

It wasn't any shortage of qualifications that decided Marshak against Drummond. He simply saw him as a wimp. Over a traditional tattersall patterned hunting shirt, he wore a dark wool jacket, and his dark trousers looked like sixteen-wale cords. He was close to sixty years old, Marshak judged, and about five nine, with a well maintained build. His complexion was florid, and he had the sort of face that aged obligingly, gentle folds developing around his mouth where Marshak wore harsh parentheses.

Oh, he knew the type. Drummond retained a look of old English traditionalism, a kind of tweedy uniformity that went out in the '60s and projected a sense of extraordinary self-control. He would be reserved, overly analytical, slow to react... and utterly useless. Besides that, the exceptional thickness of his hair, the color of a walnut shell streaked with gray, caused Marshak to conclude that this tidy Yorkshire-type would only add to the curse of his day.

In the outer office, Marshak watched Drummond as he studied the blowups of Bonecutter, Willie Dill, Falk and Koski on the wall, the principal players in this drama. Drummond blinked once, his intelligent blue-green eyes like shutters, opening, exposing only as long as necessary to permanently record, and closing.

"I'll need to scan what you have on these individuals," he said as he headed for Beard's office. Behind him, Beard tried to fill him in on the few facts he had, including the news that they now knew that Bonecutter had been in the projection room.

"Then the FBI agents have not yet found the briefcase or explosives, Colonel?"

"No, not yet, but…"

"And they have not found the missing girl?"

"Well, no, but…"

"And do you know where the two agents are at present?"

"Not exactly. Communication is spotty from certain confines of the ship."

Walking beside Beard, Marshak muttered almost inaudibly something about how unpleasant it was, how difficult to have patience, when little insects on your back pecked away at you.

As they entered the office, Beard changed the subject by outlining what Marshak thought was an inane, elaborate plan to get Drummond on board by deploying a team of Navy SEALS he had summoned.

Marshak wondered if the Brit would see through what he himself saw as a blatant delaying tactic. Like Marshak, Beard apparently wasn't comfortable with intelligence personnel from another country—friendly or unfriendly—going on board. But, unlike Marshak, it was possible that concern for the man's safety was only part of Beard's reservation. What if the man did accidentally stumble onto Bonecutter? Or worse, found him, and the man would not relinquish control of the briefcase. A Brit would be responsible for defusing the situation, taking charge, credit and stealing Beard's thunder.

Well, Marshak decided, there was little chance of such scenarios as these playing out. Drummond would not find anything. The man would get his tidy clothes dirtied if he tried to do much digging around on the old ship.

Thumbing through the bios Beard passed to him, Drummond abruptly dismissed Beard's SEAL plan. "I'm afraid that won't do, Colonel."

Marshak, seated in a chair beside him, was silent, but he allowed that he had expected a more pussyfoot approach on the Englishman's part.

Beard, apparently unsure he heard Drummond correctly, said stiffly, "Excuse me?"

Drummond leaned forward. "With all due respect, Colonel, what you suggest would take, I estimate, at least a couple of hours to accomplish. I don't have time for such bloody shenanigans."

Marshak looked at Drummond. He had delivered that last line like Maggie Thatcher saying to the first President Bush before Desert Storm, "Economic sanctions are all well and good, Mr. President, but when do we bomb the bastards?" Marshak kept a stone face, however, not ready yet to declare his position, though he enjoyed seeing Beard redden.

"But I have my orders," Beard blustered. "And I'm afraid I must insist."

"No, Colonel." Drummond stood. "I must insist." His eyes turned cold and stormy. "Several hours ago I received a phone call from the Prime Minister. I was at an important counter-intelligence conference in San Francisco but was obliged to abandon it and fly here. I have only a few hours in which to perform the almost impossible task of finding and neutralizing a small briefcase of chemicals on a very large ship.

"I was told that you and the local authorities would have the potential bomber and his bombs in custody and have the situation in hand, but nothing seems to be in hand."

Beard opened his mouth but didn't get a word out.

"I understand," Drummond went on, "that the ordnance is set for detonation at eight o'clock tonight." He turned and marched to the door. "Frankly, I don't give a tinker's damn what your orders are, Colonel. Mine are to do whatever is necessary to accomplish what I have come here to do."

Beaming his icy blue-green eyes on Marshak, he said, "Captain, may I have a moment of your time?" and left the office.

All right!

Marshak was out of his chair and out the door before Beard had a chance to close his mouth. Marshak mentally swallowed every derogatory thing he'd ever said or thought about misplaced British reserve. Here was a Limy with balls who just might get something done.

In his office, he offered Drummond a seat, but the man declined.

Drummond reached into an inner jacket pocket. "I have something of yours."

An odd, uneasy feeling crept through Marshak as Drummond produced a large, familiar manila envelope. Its front bore Marshak's scribbled name, and he recognized it immediately as the envelope for which he had earlier turned his office inside out.

Drummond handed it to him, explaining that he found it in

the restroom he had visited when he arrived. "It was sandwiched between two strikingly pictorial magazines," Drummond said matter-of-factly.

Two burning emotions flooded Marshak, a sense of relief so profound that his entire upper torso inflated and deflated with it; but also underlying panic. He had an intuitive feeling about Pete Powers' fucking envelope, but he had not paid it proper attention early on. One should listen to the whisperings of intuition. He must have inadvertently scooped up the envelope with his magazines when he made an earlier trip to the can. Damn stupid unprofessional oversight.

"Are you aware of its contents, Captain?" Drummond asked.

Marshak didn't answer, but went to his desk and eased into the chair. Taking the envelope in his hands, he pulled the two attached metal fingers up and flipped open the flap.

Stuck to a large, folded, white paper was a small, yellow note imprinted "From the Desk of Pete Powers." Scribbled on it were a few sentences:

Captain Marshak: Sorry you couldn't see your way clear to let Norm and me on the ship to talk to Jack. I hope you don't regret that decision. In any case, here are two items I found in Jack's apartment this morning. I hope they will be helpful in some way. Have a nice day.

Powers' signature on the bottom was a distinctive scrawl beside a hastily drawn smiley face.

"Shit!"

Marshak's stomach tightened as he remembered the chopper crash. Man, he was not having a nice day. Not at all.

He removed the stick-on note from the large sheet, and as he unfolded it, his day got even worse. It was a cross-section of the Queen Mary. Spasms in his gut told Marshak that the circles in red ink were the locations of Bonecutter's bombs, pinpointed so clearly that all but a blind man, or someone who was letting the little pests on his back get to him, could have seen. He might have had bombs and bomber in custody hours ago.

He was almost afraid to look up at Drummond, but he had to know. "Has anyone else seen this?" It would be the end of his career if the Chief or Beard knew of this negligence. He had reamed Sergeant Wilson a new asshole just for allowing reporters into Com-Cen earlier today.

"No." The blink of Drummond's eyes as he replied was compassionate, but there was steel behind it.

Marshak's mind raced ahead, trying to imagine a way to salvage this situation, but he could think of none, however, he regarded the fact that the Brit had not revealed the knowledge to anyone else as another plus for the man. He had a hunch, however, that he was about to pay the price of that conspiracy.

He glanced again at the note. "Powers indicates two items."

Drummond dipped into his jacket again. "Yes, this was also in there." He offered a slightly bent, sepia photograph.

Marshak glanced at, then turned the picture over and read the notation there: Angus Bonecutter, 1934. He flipped it back to the obverse and studied it. There seemed nothing extraordinary or unique about the photograph.

Jack Bonecutter's ancestor stood on a partially constructed section of the ship's wheelhouse, obstructing most of the view of the chart room behind him. The floor of the small room in back appeared to be in mid-construction, since only the upper torso of a worker in the background was visible, the lower part of his body disappearing beneath the floorboards.

Drummond reached and retracted the picture. "I need this, Captain. It's trying to tell me something."

It flashed across Marshak's ever-expanding mind that hunches frequently played a part in the everyday lives of most individuals he met in his line of work. Oh, they would deny it, probably. They would insist that they dealt only in cold, hard facts, and that unreliable, unscientific intuition was the softer gender's domain. And yet, daily, they gambled their lives on it.

"Captain Marshak, you must help me get on that ship, straight away."

Marshak wasn't sure he had heard correctly. "Me. But, I can't get you on."

"Yes, you can." Drummond leaned forward, spreading his hands on the desk.

"But how can I?"

"Just do as I say." He turned and started for the door.

They hurried from his office and down the hall, where they stopped briefly at the photocopy machine to duplicate Bonecutter's cross-section of the ship. Drummond described his plan as it seemed to spontaneously form in his mind.

Marshak couldn't believe he heard right, and that he was actually abetting the man, but he waved away a couple of police officers that came up to them. Too late he saw his years of service, the pension and 401K going down the drain.

"Drummond, you can't do this," he whispered.

Holding a wide black marker he had lifted from Marshak's desk, Drummond flipped over a two foot by two foot desk calendar and printed something on the back in huge, heavy letters.

"Do what?" he asked.

Marshak's mouth spewed out a spray of spittle as he let go an exasperated exhalation. "You can't just walk onto the ship like this."

Drummond finished printing and handed Marshak the pen. "Why not?"

As they walked across the dock toward the escalator leading to the main deck, one of LBPD's finest made a move to challenge them, but then pressed his hand-held radio to his mouth. Marshak cringed. Checking with Beard, no doubt. Man, at a time like this, one could count his friends on one middle finger.

"Because," Marshak whispered through a false, toothy grin as another policeman headed toward them, "our loony friend with the bombs has threatened to press the big button if anyone goes on board or tries to stop him. And he already knows about the kid."

"Then he should hardly care if I go on board." Drummond seemed calm, confident, insufferably G-man. "I'm not planning on trying to stop him. He's not my responsibility nor my concern."

"But he doesn't know that," Marshak insisted.

Drummond held up the sign he had crudely printed: I AM A

SCIENTIST SENT TO FIND VOLATILE CHEMICALS ON SHIP.

Marshak felt sweat trickling down his face, despite the fact that the wind was gusting and dark gray clouds streamed like phantoms across the cold sky. He whipped his rumpled handkerchief from his hip pocket and swiped it across his face.

"But that's just it, Drummond," he said. "According to Beard, these are not your ordinary, run-of-the-mill, HAZ-MAT volatile chemicals. And you have no idea where in the belly of this old battle-ax they're hidden. It would take days."

He continued to grin nervously as he spoke, unsure as to why he felt compelled to try to impart a sense of normalcy to the insanity that was unfolding. And it struck him that it was just that: insanity.

"Drummond, it's too dangerous. I can't let you."

"Just keep walking." Drummond, too, smiled unnaturally at the policeman who neared.

Marshak waved away the officer with rising irritation.

"Look, Drummond, I can't let you put others in jeopardy just because you think you're some kind of hotshot."

Drummond stopped abruptly and turned on him with only slightly controlled ferocity. "You owe me, Captain. Big time," he stated, and resumed his brisk stride.

"Shit," Marshak hissed through gritted teeth. "I'm a dead man."

He sighed resignedly. But no matter; they were at the Up escalator now, which was still, having been deliberately disengaged earlier. There was no going back.

"This is Agent Simon Drummond," Marshak told the police officer and the quizzical security guard stationed at the base of the unmoving stairs. "He's an expert in various systems on the ship. I'm clearing him to go aboard."

The guard frowned. "But, sir…"

Marshak turned to Drummond, talking fast. "Don't forget, Bonecutter will pick you up on a monitor when you reach the gangplank at the top of the escalator. He may not be able to read that sign of yours, but if he is in fact watching the monitors, it may make him curious enough to hold off on any snap judgment."

The agent nodded impatiently. "Right."

"And you'll be sure to give Agent Falk the photocopy of the cross-section so that he can begin to look for the bombs."

"Yes, yes." Drummond patted the breast pocket of his jacket. "It's here." He turned and marched up the escalator to the gangplank.

Turning to the still protesting guard, Marshak grumbled, "Officer, it's a done thing. I take full responsibility." Turning back to where Drummond stood, he watched.

Holding up the handmade sign, the Brit stood still for a beat, then turned slowly, to be certain Bonecutter, if he did observe this bizarre proceeding, could have several views from which to read it. Then Drummond tossed the scribbled sign over his shoulder. It zigzagged down to the dock, coming to rest at Marshak's feet just as Drummond stepped off the gangplank onto the deck.

After a moment of benediction to the man's courage, Marshak

bent, picked up the sign, folded it, and stuck it into his jacket pocket. Suddenly he was heatedly conscious of the media's eyes on him, their videophones and cameras and zoom lenses atop the vans behind the barricades, straining to see him. Beard's Lieutenant Smothers would have his hands full, fielding a new round of questions from the press people who saw Drummond board the ship. Better Smothers than Marshak.

A gust of wind whipped across his face and he realized that the it had abruptly risen, thrumming wildly through flags lining the rigging of the ship behind him. The sea had turned gray. Boiling swells began sucking at the pier.

Looking up, he noticed how dramatically the sky had changed from earlier in the day. At eight, maybe ten, thousand feet above sea level, a layer of stringy cirrus clouds had formed and streamed overhead. Over the next few hours, they were entirely replaced by dark, foreboding cumulonimbus clouds taller than the width of the horizon. An early darkness would fall soon. He said a silent prayer for those on the ship.

Approaching the command post, he wanted to call his wife, but decided the call would have to wait; two of Beard's elite crew were heading his way. Maybe once he produced the original cross-section that was in his hip pocket, Beard would be forgiving enough not to bring him up on charges of negligence. Maybe. He almost laughed out loud. Who the fuck did he think he was kidding?

By the time he got to Com-Cen, darkness engulfed the ship and a cold, driving rain begun.

# Chapter 35

Quintero had received four commands from his patron in Panama City. He planned to obey three.

"Si, Senor," he had replied when commanded to go to Isla Contadora to discover the hiding place of the magical briefcase, and kill the gringo once the secret place was known.

Unfortunately, he didn't learn the hiding place, but he had a plan to do so. At least the gringo who had stolen Quintero's smile was dead; that alone warmed Quintero.

"Si, Senor," he repeated when told to fly to California and to get on the big ship, no matter what measures that required, and to find the important briefcase.

El Pulpo, the octopus that curled into every eddy of every major civilization throughout the world, had many tentacles and controlled a jet plane that regularly flew legitimate businessmen associated with various Panamanian corporations from Latin America to North America and back. Quintero had availed himself of this expediency in the past and did so this day.

He left Panama City by ten in the morning, landing at Long Beach airport at six p.m. Pacific Standard Time. He drove a rental to Long Beach, arriving at the dock at six-forty. He had done what it took to get on the ship: Overpowering a security guard in the "B" parking lot, he donned the man's dark blue jacket and cap and stuffed the guard's body into a shed at a remote corner of the lot, then slit the guard's throat.

Quintero draped his own flight jacket over his arm and tucked his beret into a pocket. The area was dark enough between spaced light standards to allow the shadows to obscure his face. He slowly, casually ambled through the "A" lot and headed in the direction of the ship.

For several minutes he mingled among the maze of other security personnel and police officers on the dock, few of whom seemed familiar to one another.

It was then that the young woman positioned in the glare of one of the parking lot floodlights screeched for attention, yanked up her tight sweatshirt, and bared her breasts.

Quintero had chosen her quickly but carefully several minutes earlier. The coed with a USC shirt had initially refused Quintero when he humbly approached her in the outer parking lot, in which she and a female companion were sitting in a black Isuzu Trooper. Quintero did not attempt a smile. The resulting grimace would surely have spoiled his plans. His manner was unthreatening, even ingratiating, and he peeled off three twenties from a roll in his pocket.

"I am a reporter. Care to make a public statement?"

At first she ignored him, but he said, "I require only three harmless seconds of your time." He slid two more Andrew Jacksons and held them before her. At this she stopped and listened.

Quintero knew about American college students. He followed the news on television. He did not claim to understand it, but he knew that many young women in universities in America embroiled themselves in causes. Many demonstrated endlessly, passionately, against what they viewed as this or that injustice. Lately it had become the fashion to bare one's breasts in public, either to make a statement, to punctuate the *cause du jour*, or just to exhibit oneself.

When Quintero had scanned the crowd in the outer lot for exactly the right woman, he fixed on this loud redhead with a mischievous face. Small of frame, she nevertheless had the endowments Quintero required at the moment: large breasts that could be easily exposed because she obviously spurned bras. Two more bills later, a bargain was struck.

"Give me two minutes lead time," he had instructed the woman, then he surreptitiously disengaged the latch at the gate separating the front from the "B" parking lot and sauntered toward the ship, the security uniform jacket allowing him to blend unchallenged.

The student's perfectly timed screech caused all heads to turn in her direction as she ran through the gate into the nearer lot, faced the ship, and raised her shirt above her head.

Quintero saw the jaw of the guard closest to him slacken, then the man's mouth fall completely agape. *En boca cerrada no entra mosca*, silently quipped Quintero. A closed mouth catches no flies. Quintero had a sense of humor.

The girl's breasts were only visible for the three Mississippis for which Quintero had asked, which he thought she counted off in her head. Blanched beneath the fluorescent lights, her breasts were glorious, large round mounds that Quintero thought, to the touch, would resemble two silken sacs of mercury. She recovered herself, turned, and raced back to the Isuzu, which leaped forward as her companion hit the gas, and they were gone.

Police and security personnel in the area probably looked at each other, raised their eyebrows and grinned. Some may have shaken their heads at what seemed a harmless college prank. An attempt at fifteen seconds of public notoriety. But Quintero did not see the aftermath of the redhead's expensive stunt. During the distraction, he swiftly slipped onto the staircase astern and darted down below to an old engine room.

"*Si, Senor*," Quintero again answered with instant accord when given the third command from el Patrón in Panama earlier today.

Two American agents on the ship must not be allowed to take possession of the briefcase, and must not live to identify Quintero, who could be traced to El Pulpo. One of the agents, he knew, was a woman. Quintero would have to find steel in his belly to do that deed.

"Finally, *compadre*," el Patrón had said, for Quintero was at this time still his friend, "you must come directly here to Panama City with the briefcase. Bring it directly to me. Remember, do not open the case. Only find it and bring it straight to me. *Entiendes?*"

Quintero needed the passing of six heartbeats to solidify his resolve.

El patron did not like waiting. "*Entiendes?*" he repeated.

"*Si, Senor,*" Quintero finally said, but his true intention was not embodied in his reply to this last command.

In 1967, he had tried to snatch the case from the gringo on the ship. Back then, Quintero had not known, had not cared to know, what was in it. He was young and full of the fire of adventure and blindly obedient to his employer. The details of why he must do a thing were beyond the purview of his curiosity; he must simply do it.

Intervening years, however, had rendered Quintero more cautious, hence more curious, and had honed his resources. El Patrón and the two American agents were not the only persons who knew the potential of the magic weapon inside the case. Quintero, too, knew.

For more than twenty-five years Quintero had been an exemplary operative, doing as he was told, devotedly, and well. But good workers eventually come to understand the ways of those who employed them. An informed worker knew that one day he would be asked to do what he alone could do. This was the point after which he was expendable. Quintero knew that once he made his delivery in Panama City, death would await at the first corner.

He smiled inwardly. El Pulpo was unaware that there was great cause to mistrust its wandering tentacle. Quintero would not go directly from the ship to Panama for two reasons: One, he must go to confession, to the first Catholic Church he could find. Two, he knew enough about the briefcase's secret to have an idea as its international market value. Quintero had decided to become a momentary capitalist. Then he would retire.

In the engine room now, he shed the guard's jacket and cap and slipped back into his comfortable flight jacket with its warm aroma of lamb, and donned his dark beret. He decided on a simple plan to locate the case. He would follow the American male agent, who would be the most persistent searcher.

He had the man's photograph in his pocket, along with the woman's, given to him by el Patrón at the Panama airport. He would let the government man do the work and then pluck the prize from beneath his nose; that was how Quintero would play the game.

First, however, he must find the man. Nothing and no one would stand in his way.

# Chapter 36

Marshak stood beside Beard and silently cursed. For all the so-called operatives, the electronic miracles and layers of visual communication at their disposal, they were getting nowhere. Sure, he and Beard looked over the shoulders of Miller and Nakamura at screens, some of which revealed the ship projection room's bank of monitors which, in turn, were trained on various areas of the ship.

Trickle-down technology. It was amazing. But where did it get them? Bonecutter, the bombs, the little girl, and the briefcase were no closer to their grasp. And, despite Beard's earlier command to Miller and Nakamura to "Get me shipboard audio if you have to rig together two cans and a piece of string," the phones and PA system had remained silent all day.

Bob, the chief engineer, relinquished all responsibility for the audio failures, offering the opinion that this outage was not directly connected to the generators; that something must have gone awry in the high-tech area of electrical operations. Miller and Nakamura concurred, but as yet offered no solution.

The monitors they watched had picked up Bonecutter several times at various places on the ship, and Beard immediately called Falk to report the sightings. However, each time Falk and Koski reached the designated location, Bonecutter had left the area, continuing to run, helter-skelter, through the vessel, still searching for the girl.

His movements became more frantic and erratic with each passing hour. Now he had returned to the projection room. When Beard reported this to Falk and Koski, who were in the process of searching the forward sections, they started backtracking on the run.

"What's that?" Miller asked. Something had moved on one of the projection room monitors.

Marshak had seen it, a blur of movement at the bottom of the screen.

Bonecutter, too, had seen it. He leaned forward, frantically adjusting the camera angle on one of his remotes. The picture remained fairly clear as the camera dipped, revealing a long shot of a large room. Nothing moved.

"That's the First Class Grand Ballroom," Nakamura said, checking a detailed deck plan that hung on the wall by the console.

"Get me a tight shot of that room," Beard ordered, his hand on Miller's shoulder.

"No can do, sir. We don't have a camera there. We have to rely on Bonecutter's monitor in the projection room."

"There it is again," Marshak said. This time it was clearer. It was a man. Marshak turned to Beard. "Which one of your operatives is that, Colonel?" he asked, knowing full well it was neither.

Beard shook his head and remained silent.

Visible for less than ten seconds, and only from the rear, the broad figure in dark pants, brown leather flight jacket and dark beret dashed from behind one column at the perimeter of the dance floor to another. And something else became clear: this man was stalking.

"There's the girl," Beard said, his voice falling in dejection as Bonecutter's camera picked up Willie on the dance floor.

Unaware she was being followed, the girl stepped slowly, cautiously onto the stage and disappeared behind a floor-length, emerald green curtain.

"The stalker looks Latin," Marshak noted aloud. "Expensively dressed." He turned to Beard. "You have no idea who this asshole is?"

Beard shook his head negatively again, but his expression said what he didn't want to acknowledge. Marshak knew he had an inkling.

Miller said, "How in hell did he get on the ship?"

"Could have been on from the start," Nakamura speculated. "They might have just missed him in the evacuation, like they missed the Girl Scout." He paused for a second then asked, "But why would an adult want to stay on the ship?"

It was natural for Nakamura to ask that, Marshak thought. He and Miller were unaware of the "various chemical properties" on board. But that was not what pinched at Marshak's brain.

"A more important question," he said, "is what Bonecutter will do now that he knows this new guy's on the ship."

He looked at Beard and nodded and the two walked away

from the console.

"So," Marshak asked softly, "you think he's from the Panamanian cartel that's after the briefcase?"

Beard sighed. "No doubt."

Marshak nodded. "It looks like he's about to detain the girl."

He saw a spasm in Beard's Adam's apple. Marshak, too, wondered just how far the stalker's definition of detain would go.

"Nakamura," Beard said as he and Marshak returned to the console, "exactly where is that ballroom?"

"It's on the deck just below the theater and the projection room, where our friend Bonecutter is, sir."

Marshak noticed that Beard was finally showing nervousness, aware of how much more precarious the situation had just become while sand continued to sift through the hourglass.

The colonel passed a hand lightly over his forehead. "Then, on their way to the projection room, Falk and Koski will pass the ballroom?"

"Well, they're one level below the ballroom right now, sir. Two levels below the theater and projection room. If, once they're in the area, they took the elevator up one level, it would open in the corridor right outside the ballroom and, up one more level, open in the corridor outside the projection room." Nakamura looked like he was onto something.

"Of course, they probably won't take the elevator, too noisy. So they'll be relegated to the stairs from their present level to the ballroom level."

He paused and studied the blueprint on the wall, then looked back at Beard. "However, due to access to the amidships funnel at that location, that particular stairway doesn't go directly to the next, the projection room, level. They'll need to go through the ballroom, to the opposite side of the room, to catch the stairway there to the theater and projection room, sir."

"Sounds like a fire safety violation to me," Marshak mumbled.

Nakamura nodded. "I'm sure it actually is, sir. However, no one has ever…"

"Nakamura," Beard interrupted, "you're saying that Bonecutter can't go to lower levels without using either the elevator or that stairway down to the ballroom?"

"Which is where the girl and the new player are," Marshak put in, being unhelpful.

Nakamura again consulted the deck plan and answered Beard. "Actually, no, sir. Bonecutter has another option. He could go from the projection room, through the theater, out the double doors into the corridor where the elevator is, go down that corridor to a room at its end, which has a stairway leading both up and down."

"Damn! I need to let Falk and Koski know what they're up against." Beard pressed lightly on his left ear. "Falk, come in. Damn!" he repeated. "Damn it all to hell!"

"What?" Marshak queried.

"Too much static, unreliable reception, too much iron and steel." He exhaled noisily. "Let's hope that he and Koski get to that room soon."

"Hope is good," Marshak muttered; it was barely audible.

By doing everything by the Army's book, they were now reduced to hoping. Marshak was irritated and enjoying watching Beard sweat. He returned his attention to the monitor and Bonecutter's back.

"What is that bastard thinking?" he said. "If only we could read his mind. Now that he knows his demands were not complied with, that there are who knows how many others on the ship, how long will it be before he presses the button on that transmitter?"

No one spoke, and Marshak felt the energy in the room coil up a notch, winding up everyone's nerves.

"I could order bomb sniffing dogs and a SWAT team aboard," Beard growled.

Marshak cut in, "According to the note he left, he's a purist about the old ship and would be a stickler about the exact time of her demise. Sending dogs and others could prompt him to trigger his bombs. It's possible the only thing stopping him at this point is having a kid on board."

He let his words trail off and headed back to the small office where Willie Dill's quietly whimpering mother and alternately cursing and praying father awaited his latest report. What could he tell them?

He looked at his watch. It was six forty-five. If Falk and Koski didn't do something quickly, in little more than an hour Bonecutter would change the Dill family's world forever as well as his own and that of thousands of others. The ship would become an inferno, and the briefcase and its chemical properties, given the imposing storm, would be mushrooming not just over

Long Beach but over half the western states.

# Chapter 37

"He's as dangerous as a second lieutenant with a map."

It was an expression Bonecutter's fellow grunts in Nam had applied to people who were fuck-ups. As in any war, Nam had its share of fuck-ups. This was how Bonecutter felt about the Long Beach Police Department.

He almost couldn't blame them. The bastards were simply inept, he thought, when he saw the Girl Scout and the man whom he took to be a plainclothesman sent to extract her from the ship.

Well, the rest of the world would soon know about the police department's incompetence. Bonecutter would do so by way of the media. He'd call a local TV station and tell them who he was; that he ordered evacuation of the ship at eight o'clock this morning; how LBPD had not complied; and how their negligence put the life of a little girl and others in jeopardy. The news networks would eat it up.

One phone call disclosing the contents of his note, which he was sure the police had withheld from the press, would put the pressure on, big time. But would it end up being too much pressure? With the press, things could fly completely out of control. Maybe it wasn't such a good idea after all. Once the news hounds got some fresh meat, the situation could change drastically and rapidly. Bonecutter had seen numerous incidents in the past that were adversely affected by media involvement.

Those situations were no longer able to play out naturally. No matter how broad their spectrum may have been, media accelerated, exaggerated, compressed, dissected, and finally distilled events into the worst that was in them. No, leaking anything to the press right now wouldn't do. What was he thinking? He wasn't thinking straight.

Then suddenly he forgot about the girl and the man and became increasingly conscious of an eerie feeling that had plagued him since he returned to this room, an inner sense that he was being watched. As he concentrated on the notion, the feeling intensified, prickling the back of his neck at first then hammering with metallic percussion on his spine.

He scanned the computers on the desk, the facing walls, rows of narrow shelves containing a radio, schematics, and miscellaneous electronic equipment. Nothing. Pushing away from the console, he hurried around the room, surveying the back wall, pausing only momentarily to note the barometer that hung there. It read twenty-nine-point-nine and dropping. He had no exterior access, but several of the external monitors indicated that rain was falling. Hard.

Moving on, he detected nothing suspicious until he glanced up at the ceiling, and there it was. Cleverly concealed where the molding met the wall opposite the desk was a slit of lens, wide-angled, capable of taking in the entire room. Obviously, part of the first-class security system, a monitor monitoring the monitor.

"*Quis custodiet ipsos custodes?*" he quoted. Who shall keep watch over the guardians? That camera must have cost them a bundle.

Snatching a marker from the desk's surface, he climbed onto a chair beneath the lens. He uncapped the thick felt tip and tested it on the wall. Then, stretching up, slowly and deliberately, enjoying the screech of felt on glass, he smothered the recessed lens with moist, black bands of ink. He couldn't help but smile at the irony of it all: a million-dollar surveillance system rendered useless by a ninety-nine-cent marker.

He jumped down. What was it he had planned to do next? He couldn't recall. Why, now when he needed to think clearly, was his mind trying to wander? Should he go back to his safe place, the bridge and the chart room? There he could forget the girl and the man who pursued her and pass the rest of his life in the womb of the ship where he belonged.

Jesus, that sounded so Oedipal. It was good that the end was near; he was beginning to sound like a fucking psycho. Marissa, who never missed an appointment with one of her analysts, would say, "You're so anal, Jack."

Marissa. He pushed aside the sliver of fear that had intermittently dogged him, that even death had not the power to cure the torment of being without her. How had all that was right gone so wrong? He put a hand to his forehead and scrubbed. A jackhammer was at work behind his right temple.

Then a glance across the monitors arrested thought and motion. A camera set up to capture close-ups of dancers in the ballroom looked directly into the Girl Scout's face. The picture was of poor quality, but it caught a curious, innocent face with huge eyes like dark brown planets of water.

His breath caught. And then it seemed she looked straight at him. Her lips were slightly parted, and he imagined he felt her warm young breath, smelled the sweetness of it, like heather warmed by the sun, breath like that of the daughter he had wished for but would never have.

His hand went to his head again. Wait. What was this in his hand? The remote. When had it jumped from his pocket into his hand? He could have accidently set it off!

His head swam and, as if it were afire, he dropped the remote back into his pocket. He felt control slipping away, his life rushing on too quickly, turning a corner he could not allow it to turn now. His eyes squeezed shut. A ringing in his ears began and rose to a roar, and he smashed his fist into the center of the console, sending shards of plastic flying in every direction. He stumbled around the room, his body ricocheting from one point to another, writhing in agony.

"Aaagh!" he screamed, his mind bruised and aching.

Flesh exploded around him. A piece of a buddy fell at his feet. Another splattered across his chest.

"No! No!"

The responsibility was not his. The Army shrink had said so. It was not his fault. But Bonecutter knew better. He knew the remorse of which he never spoke to anyone, the guilt of gladness.

Yes, he was glad, despite himself. Pleased it was not he who died; implicit in that, happy they did? That it was not his heart strewn across the minefield. Joyful, then, that it was theirs? He had never, *could* never tell anyone about his secret guilt of gladness.

Above all, he didn't allow himself to feel it. Never again, not even for an instant. To feel anything meant to be touched, to face judgment. And to face that judgment was to be forced to do something about it. They did something. They died. They gave their lives. And he, he was here. Goddammit. Alive.

His eyes closed involuntarily, opened wildly, and his mind went somewhere beyond the moon. A lyric that fell pleasantly on his ears filled the air. "Piping down the valleys wild…on a cloud I saw a child."

A child.

Jesus, God! How could he do it? What kind of monster was he? What kind of fiend kills a ten-year-old?

There was only one thing he could do. He must retrieve the bombs, all of them. Take them back to the chart room. It was not the way he'd written the last chapter, but an experienced author went with the flow. An expert did not feel the need to adhere to an original story outline but let his characters to some extent dictate their fate.

He and Pete Powers had often discussed the fact that a good writer wanted that spark, that surprising, spontaneous element that happened in the process of the race to the finish.

Bonecutter would die with his bombs in his arms. This altered means would bring him to the same end, and cure him of a life which, like that of the beached Queen Mary, lacked dignity.

But where were the bombs? His head buzzed like a chain saw.

Think. Think.

He fought the shrinking feeling, the loss of eye control.

Think, you bastard.

Then he remembered. One was in the flag cabinet in the wheelhouse of the bridge. And one was in the wedding chapel. One was in Ye Olde Bakery Shoppe. One in an engine room.

Yes, he remembered now. He spun and propelled himself from the room, out into the corridor, down to its end, and into a room where he knew a stairway led to the lower decks, where he would start a rewrite, before he met a sharper grief than death.

# Chapter 38

Double-timing up the stairs to the ballroom level, Falk stopped abruptly on the landing, and Koski rear-ended him, knocking her back against the railing, her high-tops squeaking against the top stair.

"Ssh," Falk cautioned, an index finger to his lips, breathless from the race here. He looked around with obvious disappointment. "Damn."

The landing faced a blank wall; the only exit was a door to the right.

"The stairs don't continue up from here. We'll have to go through the ballroom. There's bound to be stairs leading from there up to the next level, where the projection room is."

Koski was silent. She didn't think there was bound to be anything, but her partner always looked on the bright side.

Falk put his hand on the doorknob and slowly opened the door, his Beretta at the ready, and as he did, he felt a vibration in his jacket pocket. He shut the door.

"Damn."

"What?"

"I'm getting something but it's impossible to make out with

all the static."

Koski pressed her ear mic. "Yeah, me too. Say something."

"Like what?"

"That'll do. No static. We can still stay in contact. Seems distance and surrounds have gone crazy. Beard must have been trying to convey some news."

"It'll have to keep a while. Once we're inside," he whispered, "if you hear a sound, any sound, drop. Right?"

She nodded and he reopened the door. He dashed inside, positioning his back against a large marble column. At his left, Koski dropped to her knees, her pistol drawn.

There was a half-second of hesitation before Falk followed suit. He, too, heard something. His weapon fanned the room. Nothing moved. He rose slowly.

Later he admitted to himself that he didn't like that Koski had heard the sound before he did, but now he heard and concentrated on a series of faint, muffled, thumps emanating from somewhere in the high, broad, seemingly empty room.

He signaled Koski to the left and he took the right, the two nosing cautiously into recessed areas and around the large, Italian marble columns positioned several feet from the walls.

Then the sound repeated: a thumping, louder now, like two feet simultaneously pounding the hardwood floor, yet he was still unable to pinpoint its location. Hugging the wall, he edged toward the stage he knew was behind the long, heavy green curtain. Something looked wrong. Yes, the green drape was askew, one panel had been torn away. He was close to the sound now. Slowly he pulled aside the curtain.

The stage was bare, except for a wooden, six-by-six-foot, breakaway musicians' platform at its center. Falk crept closer to the structure. The sounds were coming from under the three-foot high platform. But there was something else: a moan, a choked cry.

"Koski, " he started to call.

A faint footstep to his right made him aware that she had already skirted the room and was there at his elbow. He re-holstered his weapon and quickly examined the platform. Two metal handles were folded into a recess on one side.

"Hurry!"

Pulling the handles down, they were able to lift the framework slightly, and a fold of green curtain tumbled out at their feet. Straining with the structure's weight, they hiked it higher and yanked it back, away from the twisted, mangled mound of emerald drapery, which came to renewed life at the sound of their presence. Crouching beside it, they began tearing at the material.

The large hazel eyes were what Falk saw first, and they shimmered with a circus of emotions. Then the rest of Willie Dill was revealed. Gagged with a stiff peach-colored linen napkin from the adjoining galley, her lips were cracked and slightly bloodied at the corners. Koski started loosening the knot, while Falk untied similar linens that bound the girl's wrists and ankles.

Her mouth finally free, Willie's chest expanded convulsively, her lungs enveloping a great draft of air, then expelling it with a groan. She flung her arms around Koski's neck and cried hysterically.

"It's okay," Koski soothed. "You're okay now, Willie." She rocked the child in her arms.

Falk reached over and patted Willie's shoulder as her tears began to subside. "Are you hurt?"

She touched her lips, still breathing spastically. "Only my mouth, from the napkin."

Falk looked at Koski. "Why would Bonecutter do this? It's uncharacteristic."

"What happened, Willie?" Koski asked.

She shook her head and dabbed at her lips. "I didn't see much. A guy grabbed me from the back. He was a huge dude."

Koski nodded. "Good. Anything else?"

"I saw his wrists. The hair was dark, almost black." She shuddered, remembering his harsh touch. "And his skin was darker than mine, like my friend Maria. She's Hispanic."

Falk and Koski exchanged glances.

"Not Bonecutter," Koski said. "I saw his photo in Beard's office when I arrived. Caucasian, blond, medium build."

Falk nodded, but his skin creeped in various places on his body. "The 'serious competition' we spoke about this morning. That must be why Beard called, to warn us that he's here on the ship."

Koski ran a hand through her hair. "Oh, God."

Falk's eyes narrowed as he thought hard. "The good news is that he, whoever he is, did not want to critically harm her, merely to keep her out of the way." He paused, and his eyes twinkled as he leaned close to Koski and whispered, "Not a bad idea, really."

"Yeah, right." Koski rolled her eyes. "But, seriously, what do we do now?"

A sharp flash of lightning strobed the room and the floor reverberated with the storm's first thunderous display. Willie closed her eyes, and made an almost imperceptible shuffle closer to Koski.

The next moment a piercing, animalistic "Aaagh!" resounded directly above them and echoed through the neighboring rooms and corridors.

Falk shot Koski a look of stunned disbelief. "Come on," he shouted and ran for the stairs he hoped were there.

# Chapter 39

As Bonecutter raced through the ship collecting his carefully constructed explosive mounds, he grew calmer, his determination now funneled and focused solely on his collection effort.

He no longer ruminated on reconciling the past, no longer questioned whether death would cure him of the disease called Marissa. Indeed, the very speculation as to how much of the poor, dear Queen Mary he ultimately took with him no longer entered his thinking.

He no longer even considered the Girl Scout's presence, although minutes earlier, this had impelled him on his present, altered path. In all but the narrow, concentrated effort of amassing his bombs, Jack Bonecutter had "left the building."

He halted now in the Trafalgar Square gift shop area. "Somewhere...," he said aloud, "somewhere here. But, where?"

Then a bench caught his eye and memory returned.

"There."

He rushed to the bench, reached down and extracted the explosive from its underside. He quickly, too quickly, yanked the electronic fuse receiver from the device, as he had done with the others, unaware that the receiver had snapped, leaving half of it embedded in the mound's core.

Without examination, he slipped the device into a large plastic souvenir bag he had discovered earlier and slung over his arm. Now, he believed, he had seven unarmed bombs in the bag, their disconnected receivers in his jacket pocket. There were three bombs left. But where were they? He tried to concentrate. His feet must have moved because the squeak of his shoes jarred his thoughts.

"At the bow."

He looked around. Had he said that? He must have because, yes, he remembered clearly now that one of the last three bombs was in a stateroom at the bow. The others were in the bar below the bridge, and in the wheelhouse of the bridge, tucked in with the small, square flags used in the past for signaling in accordance with International Code.

As he ran down the wide aisle between shops, not a conscious thought, but some mechanical mode of thinking decided what to do once he had all ten explosives in hand. He would make a cake. After all, today was the seventy-first anniversary of the Queen Mary's maiden voyage. It was the event he had initially planned to celebrate. He'd combine all the little gooey mounds into one large, perfect round. There were candles: the electronic fuse receivers in his pocket. He would take this cake to the very core of the ship and, embracing it, light the wicks that would begin the celebration.

# Chapter 40

Falk had to face the fact that there was no time now to get Willie off the ship. Maybe later, once he got his hands on Bonecutter. But for now, God help them, he, Koski and Willie were a team.

Frustrated by time, they scrambled into the elevator, abandoning any real hope of silent surprise. When the lift stopped and the doors opened, Falk leaned out and checked the corridor in both directions, then headed for a door with a small window, behind which he believed was the projection room.

He peered in, a quick scan of all four walls revealing that Bonecutter, if in fact he had been there and discharged the scream they heard minutes ago, was gone. Falk silently cursed. It must have been him. He pushed open the door. Maybe their prey would show up on one of the screens on the desk.

Willie followed him in, but Koski stationed herself in the hallway to sound the alarm if anyone approached.

Quickly, Falk swept his vision across the screens. None of the cameras recorded movement. He noticed that a portion of the console was smashed, and shards of plastic littered the floor. Bonecutter had been here, all right. And something he saw had sent him over the edge.

A large portable radio with short-wave bands stood on a shelf at the back of the room. Falk mechanically switched it on and kept walking. Tuned to the British Overseas Service, the station filled the room with the strains of Grieg, a selection from Peer Gynt Suites. Peer Gynt, a man who went through life with no grasp on reality. Leave it to the BBC to come up with appropriate music.

Inadvertently, he moved the dial as he went to turn off the radio, and picked up an announcer forecasting the local weather: storm warnings from Point Conception to the Mexican border. Thunderstorms, unusually violent, expected to bring a fierce electrical display and torrential rains, causing high tides and winds gusting up to seventy miles per hour along the California coast and as far south as Baja.

Willie, sitting at the desk that supported three computers, seemed to be paying little attention. Falk switched off the radio, but a thrill of excitement ran through him. Finding it might have been a stroke of good luck. Here was a not just a workable receiver but a potential transmitter.

He was familiar with short-burst transmissions, a system used and perfected by the British during the Falkland Islands War. If the radio could be tuned to the frequency of Bonecutter's remote detonator, he could have someone at dockside arrange a jamming signal to respond to the same phase, and broadcast it throughout the ship.

No one would know. The signal would be pitched beyond the range of human hearing. It would allowed the entire ship to function as a tuning fork, jamming all other signals on the vessel, and rendering Bonecutter's remote useless.

Falk sighed. There was one big problem: He didn't know the frequency at which Bonecutter's remote was set. Moreover, in attempting to discover that frequency, it was possible that he might trigger the bombs. He cursed silently as he discarded the idea.

"Willie, what are you doing?" He realized that she had booted up all three computers.

"Don't get tweaked," she lectured. "Didn't you say that the phones and PA system are still not operational?"

"Yes, but…"

"This will only take a second." She had already determined the last function performed on each of the first two computers and was working on the third. "This might help us."

Her fingers flew over the keys, yet she maintained a steady stream of chatter as she alternately clicked her way to various windows and admonished the tortured machine for being too slow to respond or for not obeying her commands.

"Settings," she ordered as she tapped a key. "Drive converter," she directed, striking several others.

The entire operation took place in mere minutes, during which time Falk unsuccessfully protested.

"Aha!" she exclaimed as she kept tapping. "This is basic, elementary, Computer 101 stuff. Looks like they were in the process of converting the file system when the power failure occurred, or when they had to evacuate. What a nightmare for them."

She paused as if she expected Falk to ask her to explain further, and when instead he tried again to protest her actions, she ignored him and answered the unasked question as she worked.

"To save information on files, a computer uses a filing system to control how the files are stored on the hard disk."

She punched another key and several windows opened simultaneously, cascading down the screen. Falk could not have understood them if he tried, which he did not. He had an old desktop computer at home on which he played video games for dexterity, but he knew little of the machine's mysterious inner workings.

"Aha," Willie repeated. "This machine went into hibernation mode."

Again the pause. Enthusiasm compelled the technician to explain, but Falk was too frustrated to stroke a ten-year-old psyche.

"Hibernate features," she went on indomitably, "allow the computer to enter a suspend state, with all power turned off. I'll bet they tried to restart about the same time the external power failure occurred, or, more likely, when the power was restored." She paused, in deep concentration. "Still…"

Her furious clicking of keys pushed Falk to his boiling point. "Willie," he said, "you have exactly one minute, and we're out of here."

"Yes," she said, not in response to his threat, it seemed, but to some function of her work. "It looks like this hard disk is between two gigabytes and two terabytes. It could accommodate the conversion to a file system compatible with the other computers in the network.

"It'll be more efficient because it uses a smaller cluster size, which makes better use of disk space. It can relocate a root directory with backup copies, making the computer less susceptible to crashes. Goofy," she suddenly exclaimed, as if reproving the machine.

"The computer knows what it's doing," she explained to Falk. "It's people who screw things up." She talked fast as she began a final series of keyboard commands.

"So, during the system conversion, the anti-virus software detected that the boot record had changed. It offered to repair that situation. The silly person who was doing the conversion told it to go ahead and perform that repair, which he or she should definitely not have done. This changed the boot record, and the hard drive and all of the information on it became inaccessible."

She turned to Falk with an expectant, suspended expression.

"And that data included the operational codes for the PA system and most of the phone lines, which, if I'm correct, should now be..." she turned back to the keyboard and with an index finger gently tapped one key, "operational."

The phone on the desk did not ring but gave a slight half-jingle as if goosed. Falk picked it up, and, getting a dial tone, stared at the girl, his mouth open.

"It's working."

Willie smiled broadly, her small, even teeth a toothpaste-commercial white, the crinkle of her cheeks partially closing her hazel eyes behind her glasses.

"Willie," Falk felt compelled to ask as he took hold of her arm and gently dragged her from the machine, "what kind of books do you read?"

He expected her to name computer manuals, or maybe Einstein's special and the general theories of relativity. He wouldn't have been surprised if she said she was too busy surfing the Net to find time to read.

Instead, she gave him a what-do-you-expect-a-kid-to-read look? "'Attack of the Talking Toilets'," she said. "And 'Winnie the Witch'. And I just finished 'Just as Long as We're Together' for the third time." She added, "I also like jokes and riddles."

Falk let go of her arm and she followed him toward the door that led back to the corridor and Koski.

"Can you say this tongue twister fast three times?" she asked as she walked. "Upon an island hard to reach, the east beast sits upon his beach. Upon the west beach sits the west beast. Each beast thinks that he's the best beast. Which beast is best? I thought at first the east beast was the best and the west beast was the worst. Then I looked from west to the east, and I liked the beast on the east the least."

Falk raised his eyebrows and silently kept walking. At the door, he turned and shot a final glance at the surveillance screens.

"Hold on."

Where there had been no movement earlier, several cameras now recorded a flurry of motion. A blond male dressed in jeans, a black turtleneck sweater and denim jacket, raced down a long hallway bordered by souvenir shops, heading toward the front of the ship.

"Bonecutter," Falk whispered, and his heart leaped. Now he'd get the bastard.

"That's Trafalgar Square," Willie squealed. "That's where I hid in the gift shop behind the rack of T-shirts."

She paused only for a second, then asked, "Who's that other guy?"

Falk had seen him. The camera angle was poor and the interior area ill-lit, but Falk made him out to be late fifties, with a tweedy, conservative look. He was definitely not Hispanic. He was in the officers' quarters, diligently checking lockers and old chests of drawers.

The man moved smartly, nimbly, with the quick thoroughness of a pro. A practiced burglar who enters one's home must hustle to locate the greatest number of treasures in the shortest period of time.

He never opens the top drawer of a dresser first, because he would then need to close that drawer in order to inspect the contents of the second, and so on. He opens the drawers from the bottom up, leaving each open as he moves on to the next one above it. Yes, this man was professionally trained.

The MI6 agent, Falk concluded. But how did he get on the ship without Bonecutter seeing him on a screen in this room? Or maybe he had. Maybe that sight had precipitated the agonized scream they heard earlier.

Surely, Bonecutter, that poor, deranged son of a bitch, was now on his way to the place where he would detonate his bombs. He could have done it with the remote from here, but no. Falk's original hunch may have been right.

To the extent possible, Bonecutter would stick to ritual, carefully choosing a particular room in which to die, a symbolic place.

Falk grabbed Willie's hand. A glimpse at one monitor had let him see the dark, wind and rain they would encounter once they reached exposed portions of the promenade deck on their way to the gift shop area.

He was about to remove the thicker jacket from under his rain jacket and put it over Willie's shoulders, when he spotted a limp, black leather-look jacket hanging on a hook near the door, its folds gathering dust.

"Here," he said, swinging it down and around her, hardly taking notice that it was a man's large size and that Willie nearly disappeared beneath it.

"Come on. You'll have to run to keep up with Koski and me."

He would insist, when they got to the forward gangplank, that Koski take the girl and go down to the dock. Now he shouldered the door to the hallway, prepared to thank Koski for her uncharacteristic patience.

# Chapter 41

When Falk and Willie had entered the projection room, it had taken Koski less than two minutes to grow tired of waiting in the hall. Waiting was not one of her strong subjects. Particularly idle waiting. As a general rule, to make any period of waiting more tolerable, she usually did at least one other thing while she waited.

In a doctor's or dentist's office, she read or knitted. At home she seldom did one thing at any given time. When she watched a video (or on the rare occasion when she caught a show on television), she also read or wrote in her journal or knitted.

Outside the projection room, she quickly grew antsy, pacing the floor. Her stomach growled, reminding her that she was hungry, and she reached into the pocket of the tee beneath her sweater and extracted a power bar.

She had nearly finished it when she heard something that caused her to turn, and saw a door closing at the end of the long corridor. Someone had started to enter the passageway, had seen her and changed course. Without thinking, she bolted in the direction of the suspicious door.

Racing down the long artery, she drew her Beretta. She did

not know if the phantom she was pursuing was Bonecutter or Willie's attacker, but she guessed Bonecutter. Wouldn't the man who was after the briefcase have stopped and confronted her? A man strong enough to lift the corner of the heavy musician's platform in the ballroom and drag it over Willie's bound body would not run from Koski. It had to be Bonecutter, running to elude her. Well, she was prepared for whomever. She hefted the automatic.

There was a time when the mere thought of carrying a gun scared Kosk;si to death. That changed when she excelled in marksmanship at Quantico, and full knowledge of a pistol fostered confidence in the spectrum of its applications as a deterrent. But it was not at the FBI Academy that she gained true respect for a gun's killing qualities. She had learned that on a dark, isolated stretch of highway in Nevada when she had killed her first man.

"It's okay," Falk had whispered. "It's all right."

But it was months before she could put the killing out of her mind, and she wondered if she would ever be truly okay with it.

Kosksi stood behind the door through which the phantom had disappeared. She was confident but strained. She listened. Hearing nothing, she burst through, leveling her weapon. There was no one. She was in another narrow corridor, nearly one hundred feet in length, and complicated by dozens of intersecting doors, which she took to be individual cabins.

She stood for a long moment, listening. Silence was all, at first, but then a shoe surrendered a slight squeak somewhere ahead, and she heard the muffled but definite sound of movement.

Slowly she made her way down the passage, cautiously opening each door, scanning every cabin, and when she reached the last, saw that it had a second door, which was ajar. Stealthily, she approached the door and pushed it open, and the maze she had gotten herself into deepened. She was looking at yet another, identical corridor. She took a deep breath.

She knew that their phone ear-buds were receiving erratically, but she tried again to reach Falk and heard a steady hissing sound broken with intermittent static. Falk had his hands full. Now he alone was responsible for Willie and the briefcase. She knew he would surmise that his partner did not abandon her post outside the projection room frivolously, that she had probably found Bonecutter.

As she continued her search, always just ahead was the occasional squeak of a leather-soled shoe.

# Chapter 42

"That was a stroke of genius, Captain."

Colonel Beard patted a sodden Marshak on the back and pumped his hand as the latter, flanked by two equally drenched officers, entered Com-Cen, coming in from the cold wind and the rain.

"What made you think of it? Letting Drummond simply walk onto the ship with that sign. Who'd have believed that such a simple strategy would work?" He shook his head incredulously. "Sheer genius."

Marshak nearly went limp with surprise. Beard wasn't homicidal. Pissed even. Beard thought that he, that he…what?

Miller rose from the monitors. "Awesome," he said and gave Marshak a high-five.

Nakamura handed him a large, white handkerchief to dry his bald pate and the narrow band of dark curls that ringed his head just above his ears.

"Way to go, Captain," he said.

*What exactly have I done*, Marshak asked himself, and turned to Beard. "Sorry I didn't have time to run it by you, Colonel, escorting Drummond to the ship that way. I realize it was not part of the plan."

"Sheer genius," Beard repeated, ignoring Marshak's awkward apology, and returned to the monitors.

Marshak nodded numbly. He didn't know what was going on, but maybe this was a good time, while he seemed to be on an inexplicable roll, to reveal the crucial cross-section that was in his hip pocket and indicated the location of Bonecutter's bombs.

Of course, he'd have to 'fess up' that he'd had it all day, had lost it, and that Drummond found it in the can, and used it to blackmail Marshak into aiding him. This would not be an easy confession, but he had to do it. He cleared his throat and lowered his head slightly. "Colonel Beard, there's something I've got to…"

"Take a look," Beard interrupted, pointing at the bank of screens. He was practically gleeful. "It's working, all right. Your plan is working."

Marshak looked at the monitors. One, a shot of the bow of the ship, evidenced the ferocity of the storm that now raged through the area. Another picked up reporters and cameramen packed into the temporary tent shelters that had been set up for them near the front gate. A third displayed Simon Drummond in the officers' quarters, below the bridge, searching.

They saw Falk and Willie as they raced through rooms and passageways in the direction of Trafalgar Square. Falk showed characteristic grooves deepening between his eyebrows. Willie was nearly buried under a slick black coat. Neither Koski nor the Latin man was visible.

Marshak turned quizzically from the screens.

"Look," Beard persisted, pointing to a particular monitor that intermittently came alive. "Thanks to your brilliant strategy of letting him know by way of the note that there are volatile chemicals on board, the crazy bastard is retrieving his bombs."

Marshak squinted at the screen. "Holy shit!" he whispered.

It was true. There was Bonecutter, a plastic Queen Mary souvenir bag slung over his arm, pulling a mound of explosives from the underside of a bench in Trafalgar Square.

Still stunned and confused, Marshak turned to Beard.

"We can't profess to fathom the deranged mind," Beard said as if he fathomed exactly that, "but your hunch was right on. This chemical factor has thrown him. He doesn't really want to destroy anyone but himself and the ship. He doesn't fancy himself as a murderer. So he's gathering the bombs. Probably devising a new plan. But at least this buys us some time."

He turned to Miller. "Try Falk again. I've got to get this news to him."

"Now that the phones are working," Miller said, "we can call him, sir. Or use the PA system."

Beard ran a finger across his thin upper lip. "No, Miller. At this sensitive time, when he's collecting the bombs, I don't want to take a chance on alerting the bastard to the fact that Falk and Koski are on the ship, in the event he doesn't already know."

Slowly Marshak began to comprehend his luck. He breathed deeply and straightened his shoulders. Maybe, hey, subconsciously, he had this fortunate turn of events in mind all along, as Beard accredited. Maybe, on some subliminal plane, he instinctively knew that Bonecutter would react in this manner.

Yeah, and maybe pigs fly.

In any case, he doubted that this would change Bonecutter's mind about destroying himself and the ship at the prescribed time. He remembered Norman Chaum's words from this morning: "The first bomb that goes off may be in Jack Bonecutter's head. You may get your explosion before you expect it."

If poor, bomb-infested Bonecutter and the briefcase met and ignited at any time, in any part of the ship whatsoever, a huge chunk of humanity would go with them.

Touching Marshak's elbow, Beard steered him to the other side of the room, his voice lowering to a near whisper. Marshak figured he'd had all the accolades he was going to get from the good colonel this day."Captain," Beard lightly squeezed Marshak's biceps as he spoke, "from Bonecutter's reaction to Drummond and the note, it appears that we were, ah, wrong when we tried to delay the Limy's access to the ship earlier."

Beard's eyes narrowed as he looked into Marshak's. "Or, is it possible that I misremember that the Navy SEAL operation we had planned might not be viewed after the fact as a delaying tactic at all? How do you see it, Captain?"

Marshak savored a long moment of sweet comprehension before he said with obvious magnanimity, "Actually, Colonel, I don't recall any such plan."

Beard released his muscle and slapped his shoulder. "Good man." He immediately turned his attention back to the monitors.

Marshak stood alone for a full minute. So Bonecutter was

collecting his bombs from where he originally hid them. Man, it was funny how things sometimes worked out.

He jammed the hopefully-forever-moot cross-section farther down into his hip pocket and wondered if he could talk Drummond into doing the same with his copy. True, his problems were far from over, but maybe not all of the wiry, highly charged energy of the day had worked against him.

# Chapter 43

Stealth and cunning, two qualities Quintero had in abundance, were needed to stay ahead of the tenacious young woman with hair the color of a collie he owned as a boy in his abandoned homeland of Venezuela.

At first, Quintero's plan had been to follow the male American agent, who he initially believed would lead him to the briefcase. But the Latino had judged the character of the male and found it to be lacking, evidenced by his release of the child Quintero had waylaid, then by allowing himself to be saddled with two females.

Quintero concluded that he would do better to separate himself from what he saw as an inept trio and search on his own, but then was discovered by the woman in the corridor. More like a pesky bloodhound than a collie, she had been nipping at his heels ever since.

At the same time, Quintero was torn with indecision. What should he do with this woman who would not give up, who followed him down endless hallways, through countless rooms, up and down stairways? He could easily have killed her if he made up his mind to do so. She was surprisingly prepared and acutely alert, quick in her thinking and in her physical dexterity. But Quintero, too, was all of these, and more. Quintero had manpower.

Hidden behind a door, he might have lunged at her, overpowered her, and snapped her neck in one well-executed twist. But that meant explaining that death to the Catholic Padre tomorrow. How could he justify another life-taking this day, especially that of a woman?

Time raced on. Quintero's desperate mind was on the threshold of formulating a motive that he believed to suffice in the confessional, when an alternative plan presented.

# Chapter 44

In her dogged pursuit of the man she thought was Bonecutter, Koski had cautiously turned a corner into another hallway, and heard the whirring, metallic sound of an elevator.

She dashed down the long corridor and discovered that there were in fact twin elevators, the arrow on the lighted half-moon panel above one indicating that it was descending.

She jabbed the Down button of the second, fidgeting and cursing at the few seconds it took the doors to open. The other lift continued to descend to the lowest level of the ship, it seemed.

"Down," she demanded as she rushed inside and stabbed the small red button.

Ten decks later the doors opened into a narrow passageway, at the end of which was a door with a red metal sign printed in faded white letters: Boiler Room.

The twin elevator's doors shut. Koski looked up and down the passage but saw no other door.

"Aha!" she whispered. "Now I've got you, Jack Bonecutter."

She approached the boiler room door, Beretta in hand, and it flashed through her mind that, yes, she had him; but since there was only one way out of this passage, he had her, too.

She took a deep breath, turned the doorknob, and burst into the room, swinging her back to the wall and fanning the width of the room with her pistol. Then she dove for the only cover available, a huge chunk of rusted, indistinguishable machinery on the floor.

Two small, amber lights at shoulder height on opposing walls cast dim, dawn-like light and created long, eerie shadows around the room, whose size seemed to swallow her.

Trained to marginalize risk in such situations, she peered through crevices in the antiquated metal she'd chosen as cover. She scanned the area for another exit, keen to any sign of movement and saw a door at the opposite end of the room.

Good.

The air in the room held cool, uncanny silence. It was a dank room, more than twenty feet high, and broad. The boilers had long since been removed; the room had gone to wreck.

Ruined pieces of equipment—a portion of an anchor, rusted chunks of chains and pulleys—littered the gutted expanse. Some resembled sleeping cats, some armored armadillos.

Slowly she rose, convinced that she was alone in the room, and began crossing to what she both hoped and feared would be the final door. Then she halted. She had heard a slight click behind her. A dark moth fluttered in her chest.

No! No!

She whirled around and raced to the door she had entered moments before, grabbed the knob and turned and pulled. And pulled. It was locked!

Oh God!

She kicked furiously and pounded it.

"Bonecutter!" she screamed. "Bonecutter, you bastard, let me out of here!" She kicked again, as if kicking herself. A stupid, rookie mistake. "Bonecutter!"

It was the twin elevator. She should have checked the other out. He must have been hiding in it, waiting, as she exited and, like a lemming going to the sea, entered the boiler room, which was now her prison.

"Damn."

She kicked again. She'd been outsmarted. Another kick, then she stopped and listened. A muffled, grating sound. One of the elevators was ascending

*The motherfucker is leaving me here.*

She froze, an inhalation lodged in her lungs, and listened again. Slowly the sound faded, and she knew then she was truly alone in the silence.

Perspiration broke out on her face and palms. She swung around to face the room, her tomb. But, wait, she'd forgotten the other door. She darted to the opposite side of the room, unafraid of what was behind that final means of exit.

It was a way out; wherever it led she would follow. When she reached it, she grabbed the knob and turned.

It opened to an empty closet.

Or was it?

She leaned in. The dim light behind her offered little illumination and created a diagonal coal black shadow in the small chamber. She stepped closer. A musty coolness hit her, and a hollow roar assailed her ears. Jabbing a hand into her jeans pocket, she extracted a small cigarette lighter that she never used but carried.

She swiveled her head in and peered up. And up. And up.

The tiny room had no visible ceiling. In fact, it was not a room at all, but a narrow, vertical shaft only slightly wider than a human body. Wooden ladder rungs built into one wall vanished into the ascending blackness.

Lack of proper illumination disclosed only dust and cobwebs on the first dozen rungs and kept Koski from noticing the splinters of wood at her feet, evidence of fresh disturbance of the upper, unseen rungs.

Was it possible that this interior ladder went up to the next deck; or up through many decks? If so, one could avoid all stairs and elevators by utilizing this to climb all the way to the top deck of the ship. She shuddered; but what a climb.

She backed out of the chamber, a hot flash of blood flooding her cheeks as she recalled the long crawl through the conduit with Falk this morning. As bad as it had proven, she had been with Falk. She had not been alone like she was now.

She had one moment of utter, sickening fear. She could not swallow, and her entire body shivered. Then she froze with a profound realization. For her, the ladder was the only way out of this room, and there was no force on earth that could impel her to climb it.

She breathed deeply for several seconds, and then spoke into her ear mic. No use. The entire ship was full of dead spots. "Can-you-hear-me-now?"

Shit.

She pulled out her phone and texted a message, but was certain it wouldn't be received. Sweat broke out anew on the surface of her skin as, painfully, reluctantly, she let her vision drop to her watch. It was seven-fifteen.

# Chapter 45

"I hope Susan is okay." Willie breathed heavily as she spoke.

She and Falk had been racing through the interior of the ship, and now they halted beside the bench Bonecutter had been concerned with less than ten minutes before.

"I'm sure she is." Falk, too, needed to catch his breath.

The thought of time running out was as exhausting as physical activity. And, despite his encouraging words to Willie, he was not sure Koski was okay.

He hadn't a clue as to why she left her post in the hallway while he and Willie were in the projection room, but assumed she must have had a good reason. Perhaps the man who imprisoned Willie earlier had come into the hall and found her. No, Falk would have heard the sounds of the fight Koski would have waged against the man. Unless he surprised her from behind, as he had Willie.

"Look," Falk said, as if Willie had protested his attempt to assure her about his partner, "Koski's fine. She's well trained and smart and physically strong. She's fine. Wherever she is, she's just fine."

But instinct screamed the opposite at him.

"Willie," he said, "I have to get to the bridge, at the front of the ship, not far from here."

He looked around for a place to tuck the girl away, where she'd be safe but out of his hair.

"But..." she began.

"No 'buts'. This is serious business."

He turned to the nearest shop. The Press Museum. Inside he saw racks of old newspapers covered in plastic, their headlines depicting historic world and local events.

"Perfect," he said. "A newspaper museum." He tried the door, dug into his pocket for a ring of universal keys he'd been given before boarding and unlocked it. "Great for an intelligent, well-read young lady like you."

"But I want to go with you."

Falk put his arm around her shoulder, steering her toward the door. "No. This is important, national security business."

That should do it.

"But I helped you before, with the computers. I could..."

"Look," he struggled to keep his voice steady, "Willie, remember the man we saw on the monitor before, the one who was here by the gift shop?"

Her brown eyes narrowed, intense and interested. "Yes."

"Well, he's a danger." A sigh. "He's a very sick man who is confused, and I've got to find him and get him off the ship and to a doctor."

An old grandfather clock inside the museum struck, and Falk looked at it. It was seven-fifteen.

"Oh, God."

He put his hands on her shoulders and shoved her into the shop. "Stay here until I get back." He pulled the door shut and ran.

He raced down the long corridor, angry and frustrated, and the one thing he hated most—unsure. He had only questions, no answers. Where was Koski? Had she found Bonecutter? Where was Willie's attacker? Where was the MI6 agent who Beard said would assist in the search?

He tried his ear-bud. Where was the verbal communication they'd been promised? Where was the freakin' briefcase? And, finally, where had his groove gone?

He was always at his best when the challenge was greatest, when all pistons were firing. Instead, the heat of frustration burned his cheeks as he charged forward, past staterooms, the Observation Bar, heading for the exposed staircase leading to the bridge, where he hoped to get some answers.

# Chapter 46

Willie looked around the museum, unsure how she wanted to proceed. Beside her was a rack of plastic-wrapped newspapers, and she speculated that if she were going to stay here as instructed, she could pass the time by reading.

The one-word headline of a Los Angeles Times Extra dated Tuesday, June 6, 1944, read: INVASION! Willie leaned toward the rack and silently read the ensuing story: "Allied forces landed in Northern France early today in history's greatest overseas operation, designed to destroy the power of Hitler's Germany."

She moved on to the next, a Connecticut newspaper, The Torrington Register, dated Saturday, September 10, 1960. "Hurricane Donna Rakes Florida Keys" was the headline.

The front page of the Los Angeles Citizen News of Friday, November 22, 1963, had a full-page, black-and-white picture of a handsome man with thick hair, a kind face, and sad eyes under the headline: MARTYRED.

Willie turned away from the rack and looked out of the museum. She didn't want to read old news. She wanted to be where things were happening *now*. And she decided that if the man who attacked her this morning was nearby, she would be safer with Falk than here alone. She ran to the door, threw it open, and took off in Falk's direction.

# Chapter 47

Falk was drenched when he reached the bridge. Once open, the heavy door was held in that position by near-hurricane-force gusts of wind that drove through the navigational area, whining at every crevice and hurtling a thick film of rain against the surrounding windows.

His mind screamed he should have brought Willie, taken her down the gangplank, handed her to someone ashore. But he knew that unless he found Bonecutter and stopped him from igniting his bombs, it would make little difference where she was when that terrible occurrence took place. There'd be few left alive to witness the result.

A rope ladder hanging from the crow's nest slapped powerfully against its restraints. It was dark outside, but Mother Nature's aerial display and the army of klieg lights brought in by the Long Beach PD to the dock ten stories below augmented the Queen Mary's usual lighting. The ship was awash in surreal radiance, keeping total darkness at bay in some areas while creating more and deeper shadows in others.

Activity was at a standstill on the port side dock. Except for those armed, slicker-covered sentries at strategic posts, police and security personnel had taken shelter in Com-Cen or one of the temporary shelters that were set up.

Starboard, the crisscrossing searchlights of several Coast Guard vessels made silver beads on the cresting surface of the black water. They patrolled the area outside the rock jetty that separated the Queen Mary's berth from the bay.

Salvage vessels loaded with Coast Guard and National Transportation Safety Board personnel still combed the bay. They were hampered by waves that battled each other and broke on the jetty, sending whorls of water high above the rocks and slamming down, then running off in a smother of writhing foam.

Falk took only a second to shake the collar of his rain jacket to disperse some of the water that had collected and chilled his neck and shoulders. Cautiously, he scanned the bridge for Bonecutter, but there was no sign of him or anyone.

He entered the small chart room, which was deserted, and as he did, his hunch that the briefcase was somewhere in this area grew stronger. Like a bloodhound on the trail, he sniffed into every oblique corner of the room. He flung open any cabinet large enough to hold a briefcase or an incendiary bomb, checking for hidden compartments, feverishly overturning everything that was not nailed down.

One unusual cabinet contained pigeonhole compartments stuffed with old, rolled signal flags; he tapped them lightly, almost absent-mindedly in his haste to locate Bonecutter and the briefcase.

"The briefcase has got to be here somewhere," he said aloud.

The only clue he had was the old scientist's disclosure to the

FBI agent, that it was hidden where no one would find it.

A clap of thunder rolled like a heavy wooden barrel across the sky.

*Think*, his mind whispered. *And remain calm.*

Then he hated that he'd thought that. He was always thinking. He was always calm. He'd find the case, God damn it!

Looking at his watch, he realized its hands had not moved since he last looked. His fine, precision Swiss movement chose precisely the worst moment to stop working. Fate was playing another dirty trick against him.

He sighed deeply and stepped past a bulkhead, surveying the area as he went. Creaking timbers groaned, warning that something would eventually had to give. Moving to his left, he passed the large, waist-high chart table and began opening and checking cabinets and drawers in the wall facing the bay.

As he moved to the second wall, he noticed a long, low wooden bench. Did it open? He stooped and tried the seat, first pulling, then clawing at the worn, faded oak. But it was just a seat.

He stood and, with a fist, tested the wall behind the bench, searching for a movable panel, anything. But it was solid.

"Damn."

His hands flashed through every cabinet, every cubbyhole, most of which were empty, disused for years.

An instinctive glance at his useless watch exploded his frustration. He'd put his trust, his hopes in instinct—a clear sense that both Bonecutter and the case were on the bridge or this adjoining room. He'd been wrong about Bonecutter. Anxiety heightened in him. Was he wrong about the briefcase, too?

Then something drew him back to the chart table he'd passed moments earlier. On the wall above the right side of the table were framed sepia notices from old cargoes, wind velocity readings, a portion of the tidal atlas of the Solent and the approach to Southampton, England. All were scraps of paper that once were whole and held meaning for captain and crew. He moved to the left side of the table.

The bulkhead above it was battered with nail holes, and several people—no doubt tourists in recent years—had stippled their affection there: "Bob loves Carol." "Don" with a heart next to "Louise."

The shipbuilder's original name and insignia were embossed there: Cunard White Star Line, the outline of a stout, five-point star the symbol. He reached up and let his fingers read the Braille-like outline. If only these walls could speak.

Testing the area of the star, he knocked all about it for some sign of give, but no. He looked down, squatted, and realized for the first time that there was a wooden cupboard built in beneath the table.

He touched the door. It was ajar.

He opened it. The cupboard was empty, the walls solid and firm. He tapped the floorboard. At the hollow sound his tapping produced, excitement quickened his breath.

Could it be? Finding a groove in the wood, he raised one side and pushed the floorboard up against the inner wall, surprised it gave so easily after all the years. Too easily.

Dear God, if someone has been here before me...

He looked down into the black hole, the overhead light insufficient to penetrate its depth. Dropping to his knees, he began to grope gingerly inside the hole, but felt only gauzy webs. Because the section of floor opened up to the right, he had to reach in with his left arm.

He leaned farther into the unknown darkness and swept his hand under the surrounding floor, locating what felt like a ladder and three walls. Where the fourth wall should have been, directly under the portion of the floor on which he knelt, there was only space.

He dropped his body flat on the floor, face down, his left armpit crammed against the lip of the cupboard, attempting to lean farther, but his Beretta in its holster dug into his ribs and restrained his movement.

He carefully removed the weapon with his right hand, balancing his weight carefully so as not to fall into the black abyss, and slid the gun to the floor just outside the cupboard.

He was at last able to stretch in as far as he dared, fingers working, searching, locating a shelf and something else: the curved, glass neck of a bottle. It lay on its side, and he groped to position it so that he could grasp and extract it, but it swiveled, and his hand, trying to catch it, knocked it instead to the lip of the shelf and it fell.

Falk could not see but could hear its dizzying descent as it glanced off one wooden ladder rung, then another, hit the side wall of the shaft, bounced back against another rung, and continued to fall, seemingly forever.

Its motion resounded through the twelve-story chamber, until the echo grew faint and faded, evidence of its final disposition silenced by its distance from the range of Falk's hearing.

Stretching his body as far as he could now, he reached for the shelf again. His fingers touched a flat surface that felt like old, crusted leather. He held his breath as his fingers slowly crept over the perimeters of the object: a handle.

Slowly, for his arms and fingers quivered with muscle tension, he inched the handle toward him. The leather case attached to it was heavy and thick. He remembered Healey saying that the container inside the briefcase was reinforced with steel. If the steel had corroded, the chemicals begun to leak or decay, what would he do?

In desperate, intense concentration, an exaggerated vision crept across his mind, depicting his hand coming away from the shaft as an aberration of dead cells, their hideous withering spreading quickly to his wrist, his arm.

Then the case came off the shelf, its surprising weight swinging it downward, nearly escaping from his grasp. He shoved his other hand into the shaft to steady the burden, nearly toppling in himself, and carefully, in a lifetime of seconds, wormed his body back along the floor and withdrew the briefcase from the cupboard.

Breathing for the first time in minutes, his heart hammering in his chest, he got to his knees, then stood and eased his prize to the chart table.

"Aageeegh!"

The sound quivered gutturally from his throat. Violent jerks and shudders convulsed his body as he tried to fling his right hand away from himself, propelling the black, spindle-legged creature on it across the room. He shuddered several more times before he could dispel the sensation of the harmless yet repellent spider's touch.

Falk blew a layer of dust from the weathered leather and quickly inspected the case for signs of erosion that would signal leakage of the compound. He thanked God there were none. In the lower right-hand corner, burnished gold initials were recognizable: GJM. Gordon James Metcalf.

Staring at the name, he wondered how this man had been able to get into the chart room of the Queen Mary while at sea. Maybe during a shift change. Did he bribe a crew member? However Metcalf managed it, and with whom, would never be known.

Suddenly elation ran through Falk like a shot of adrenaline. He'd found it! Despite many years of action, it was still in good shape.

He remembered with irritation that Koski had in her pocket the chemical wrap in which he was to enclose the case. Well, right now, he just had to get the damned thing, and Willie Dill, off the ship and find Koski, who he hoped had collared Bonecutter.

Then, for no knowable reason, he had a chilling sense of a presence in the room with him. A vision of his Beretta flashed across his mind, and he looked down at the floor where he'd left it and prepared to bend and retrieve it.

It was gone.

# Chapter 48

Hampered by pelting rain and the gnarled shape of the plastic bag slung over his forearm, a sodden Bonecutter stumbled up the exposed stairs toward the bridge while Falk was in the chart room, extracting the briefcase from the cupboard. The door of the bridge was flung open, transfixed by the wind. Bonecutter stepped inside, slipping the plastic bag up to his shoulder.

His wandering brain no longer attended conscious, peripheral matters, and he moved mechanically, as if possessed, concentrating on the right wall just inside the bridge and a small, knee-high wooden cabinet. Inside were dozens of signal flags, stuffed into pigeonholes.

He had yanked out handfuls of flags this morning, finally extracting the one that he used to conceal his tenth and final explosive. He then replaced that flag and the others. Now he would…a strange, guttural, shivering cry came from the adjoining room, above the whine of the wind. Bonecutter took two steps forward and managed a narrow, rectangular peek into the chart room. There he saw a tall, brown-haired man in a rain jacket, wiping his hand as if something diseased had walked across it. He was examining a dark parcel on the table above the open cupboard and the shaft.

The shaft. Bonecutter's shaft. The man had discovered Bonecutter's secret place. The place where Bonecutter planned to make his cake and start the celebration.

Bonecutter whirled and flung himself back down the stairs, pinching his eyes shut against a vision that had come to him again and again in the past few hours. But he could not dispel it this time. It was there, imprinted on the inner wall of his eyelids: a malignant montage of his Bien Hoa buddies.

No!

He forced his eyes open, but now the men were there, too. Outside, standing in the rain, their uniforms in tatters, their bodies slick and bloodied, missing parts, dripping pieces. One raised a shattered finger like the backbone of a fish and beckoned to Bonecutter. The man was grinning, his mouth a gaping hole.

"No!"

Bonecutter's head tightened. His skin shrunk, crushing his skull. In whatever direction his mind turned there was no solace. Just as he put his right hand to his head, he blacked out. He came to, still moving his hand toward his face. It happened in a flash, but for the few seconds it lasted, it was complete and took a measure of his mind with it.

Twisting wildly, slammed by an icy blast of rain and wind, he stumbled blindly toward the bow. Pursued by demons, he was aware only of blood beating in his head with savage energy as he groped along the rail, tripping over an old gun platform left as a memento from World War II when his genteel ocean liner was converted to a troop ship.

Staggering to the V point of the bow, he turned back and stumbled over the windlass; his foot hooked on the mammoth chain which nearly pulled him to the deck.

Water raced down inside his clothes, soaking his skin, but he knew this more than felt it. His fingers clutched at a rail and found something—rope—the ladder leading to the crow's nest. He looked into the blinding rain, staring up at his past, knowing he had no future.

His last moment of sane, pristine clarity, told him he was being fanciful, ridiculously so. Then the vision he carried inside since he was three overcame him and became his only reality. He was, again, in that place to which he was irrevocably linked. One minute, safe in loving arms, the next flailing, a sacrifice to the wind and wild gray wolf pack. He knew only one truth: his life could not end without resolution in the crow's nest. He grabbed the ladder and climbed.

# Chapter 49

Falk looked up from the floor and saw the man who he assumed had come into the room only moments ago. He saw the taut, olive skin around an unsmiling mouth that stretched horizontally back on the right side of his face until it seemed the entire lower jawbone would be exposed. The stretch held for several seconds, then the lips quivered and the mouth closed, settling into a grim, tight line.

The man had a thick neck and massive shoulders; his torso was shaped like a sequoia, although this was not a young man. He saw the pricey, hand-finished lambskin jacket, sodden and dark with rain. But what Falk saw most noticeably was not the man himself; it was the gun in his hand. It was Falk's Beretta.

"Ah," Falk said with inherent sarcasm and controlled fury, trying to make himself heard above wind, rain, thunder and creaking, inside and outside the room. "The man who cannot smile. The man who mutilated an old man in Panama after he was already dead, and who attacked a little girl from behind and nearly suffocated her."

"*Si, Senor*," the man said. He beckoned with upturned fingers toward the briefcase. "Give to me," he said in English.

Falk didn't hesitate, his mind quickly ruling out every other possible option. This guy would kill him. He wasn't sure what time it was, but he guessed sometime between seven-thirty and eight.

If Koski failed to locate Bonecutter, it didn't matter who took the briefcase off the ship, so long as someone did. Beard's people would apprehend the man dockside. He set the briefcase on the floor a few feet in front of him and stepped back.

"Look," Falk told him, palms up in apparent surrender so as not to spook him, "it's yours. You can have it."

Did the Latin grasp the true potential of the trophy he'd won? Did he appreciate its killing power?

"Take it," Falk repeated. "Go. Get off the ship, for Christ's sake!"

Slowly, silently, the powerful man bent and picked up the briefcase, never diverting his eyes or his aim from Falk. He backed slowly to the doorway that separated the chart room from the bridge, bent again, and set the case down on the floor.

Then he made what Falk initially thought was a most unexpected move, but which later consideration proved to be evidence that his adversary was indeed wholly aware of the chemical compound's volatile potential. He placed the Beretta on top of the leather case and, in the same instant, drew a knife from inside his jacket.

Falk saw a deadly glint off six inches of cold steel as the man crouched, facing him, in the menacing, preparatory stance of a master cutter.

So, Falk thought, it wasn't only that his enemy knew of the

sensitive nature of the enclosed chemicals and was taking no chances with ricocheting bullets; this was a guy who preferred close physical contact and clean, silent strokes of a blade. He had, Falk realized in the moment, predetermined Falk's death.

The man's physique was impressive, backed up by the instincts of a professional killer. Falk would need to employ physical subterfuge to survive. If lucky, he might get one chance, one split-second opening in which to deflect a blow and to lunge and deliver, with his bare hands, a fatal stroke of his own.

Falk heard a groan—his—as the man attacked. He couldn't know that his life had been saved in that moment by a vision. In mid-thrust, an image revisited Quintero: He saw his blade, attached to the beak of *el pico de pez espada*, spinning in air. He saw his own hand stretching to retrieve it. He saw it fall, blade downturned, before the blade buried itself in his face.

The horrendous vision lasted just long enough to distort Quintero's judgment, and allow Falk to sidestep his initial thrust, which opened a gash in Falk's coat, rain jacket, his shirt, tee shirt, and a marginal layer of flesh beneath. Aware that blood had been drawn, the attacker adjusted his stance, and prepared to deliver the final assault.

Ignoring his wound, determined to invest every ounce of physical strength and mental agility into this fight, Falk yanked his rain jacket from his shoulders and whirled it around his forearm, ready for the fight of his life.

# Chapter 50

When the fragments of thick glass shattered to the floor of the open shaft, accompanied by the distinct and powerful odor of aged whiskey, it was a shocking but welcome sign of life to Koski.

Someone was up there. She had no idea who or how far up, but someone was there, and had thrown or dropped the bottle into that black hole.

Earlier her innate sense of humor had kept her from total misery. "Is this, then, the end of Susan Koski?" she'd asked aloud as she stared at the shaft, her claustrophobia gripping her in it's iron claws.

Sitting on an old piece of rusted machinery in this forgotten, high-ceilinged, hollow hell in the bowels of the ship, she fought back tears and gave in to her despair. She was on the verge of completely giving up hope for the first time in her adult life.

More than once, she played out in her mind the stupidity of allowing herself to get outsmarted and locked in this room. Hotly aware that time was running out, she felt pressure in her chest, as if a truck had pulled up and parked there.

Then the bottle had smashed to the floor, and she got up and ran into the shaft.

Now she waited and listened. There was nothing but the constant scream of air. She looked back at the huge, imprisoning room behind her, at the chunks of dead machinery covered with dust, and a vision of her bones being found here, years from now, draped over her. That moment of utter desolation finally sparked an emotion more powerful than her fear of enclosure: Rage.

"Fuck!" she hollered. "No way am I going to die here!"

She took two gulping gasps of air, as if she were about to dive into the deep end of a pool, and started up the ladder at a run, her nostrils filled and flaring with the sting of liquor.

*And if I'm really lucky*, she thought, *I'll be drunk before I reach the top.*

# Chapter 51

With a flourish, Falk's opponent swiftly, deftly brandished the knife. Falk saw it flash like sliver writing in the air. Writing his name or his epitaph? A slight light-headedness passed over him. His left hand went to his side and came away sticky with warm blood. No matter. It would take more than a flesh cut to inhibit him. He was back in his groove.

Two, three more times, the blade flashed by him; so close that his jacket was slashed to raw threads in several places. Each time his body's quick response to his mind's ability to read and interpret his enemy's movements saved him. But just as he was aware of his own capabilities, so was he mindful of his diminishing energy. How long could he hold out?

Then he heard a voice. A small voice, reaching to the top of its range to be heard above the thunder, and he saw Willie Dill standing in the doorway behind his attacker.

"Drop the knife," she demanded with a ferocity and seriousness beyond her years.

When the man tensed but did not move, not so much as turn toward her, she tightened her steady, two-fisted grip on Falk's Beretta.

"I said, drop the knife, dickoid."

Falk knew in that moment that it was possible for him to love, wholly and unashamedly, a human being he had met only hours before.

# Chapter 52

Seconds after she started to climb, instinct developed into full awareness, and Koski realized she had climbed the height of three stories. She was suddenly keenly aware of the walls on all sides and that they were nearly touching her.

She slowed and gripped harder the rungs above her, planting her feet more deliberately on each rung below. She allowed herself to think only that she felt uncomfortable, and ordered her body to keep climbing.

This worked for several more minutes, until she lost awareness of her feet and of how far she had climbed. All that existed was the screaming air above her, the sense of being unnaturally high and of being suspended in a close, smothering space.

She swallowed dryly and paused. What finally pushed her on was the thought of the blackness below, which did not recede but seemed to rise on its own like an unrelenting tide beneath her.

Now every rung was an achievement. She pulled herself painfully upward, hand over hand, foot over foot, fighting desperation, concentrating on the knowledge that there had to be an end, that she would reach the top at any minute.

Recollection of the long conduit she and Falk had traveled this morning pushed its way to the forefront of her mind. She had, for several seconds, lost consciousness then. Or had she?

Was she in fact extremely conscious, too conscious, so that the ebony darkness around her took on form—her form? It was she, her corporeal being, not her consciousness that was lost. She shook her head to clear the fantasies, prepared to shut down all her thinking processes and again ordered her body to move forward but faster.

Then a rung gave way. Then another. She began fighting her way upward to find a rung that would hold.

Every muscle was stressed to its limit. Having at last located two solid rungs, she shivered uncontrollably and clung to the ladder. Tiny slivers had imbedded themselves in her damp palms where they had desperately grasped at decaying wood, and she felt her knees and shins bleeding, scraped by the sharp remains of broken steps she had somehow climbed.

She was perspiring profusely now, and the smell of her own sweat made her stomach lurch. Bile, bitter and intolerable, convulsed into her throat, her mouth, and spilled out between her lips. Pure fear, irrefutable and paralyzing, struck her. She'd undertaken the impossible.

She could not go on. She needed to go back down, but the broken rungs ensured that she couldn't. But neither could she bring herself to continue up. The panic that was overwhelming her was like a fire, raging out of control. A voice appeared in the flames screaming at her to give up, give up.

Fingers that seemed not her own vised around the rungs. She felt a stream of warm wetness snake along her thighs and down her legs. A shudder overtook her body. Nausea welled, followed by a rush of heat and then exquisite, exhilarating dizziness. The screaming voice no longer ordered her to give up but to let go, let go.

She could feel the muscles in her fingers obeying, when, next moment a different voice refocused her senses on the looming blackness above her head. Above her, a determined child's voice boomed, "I said drop the knife, dickoid."

Koski knew that voice. It was that not far above her. Oh, God! She pressed her head against the ladder. Fear and the exertion of the long climb had robbed her of most of her strength. She tried but couldn't move.

*Oh, God, please. I can do this. I can,* she thought, but her body refused to obey.

# Chapter 53

Falk closely watched as Quintero, blade in hand, turned quickly, then back, seeming to divide his attention between the agent and the girl. Then he looked into the black orifice of the Beretta as if to gauge the determination of the brassy child behind it.

Falk, although not seriously injured, was in pain from the stab wound Quintero had inflicted. In fact, at the girl's appearance, he sank onto the long low bench against the back wall. But he would be up again soon.

Meanwhile, this little one stood less than ten feet from Quintero and demanded again that he drop his weapon. At this distance she certainly wouldn't need to be a crack shot to kill him. Still, fright or nervousness or inexperience might work to Quintero's advantage.

Falk imagined that Willie knew nothing at all about guns. Probably, she was never allowed to touch one. He remembered only half-listening as she chattered about her father who had once purchased what he called a Saturday Night Special. For the protection of his family, he had told them. In a long monologue Falk had mostly tuned out, Willie described how she watched from the hallway while her parents stood in the kitchen and examined the weapon, her father explaining how to disengage the safety lock.

"Now it's ready to shoot," he had said.

But Willie's mother always tested the depth of the water before going in. She carefully placed her trembling hand over the weapon in his and replied gently but firmly, "George, do you realize that something with killing power is in your hands? It will be in our home, where our daughter lives and plays. And you have just demonstrated to me and her how to render it unsafe."

Willie told Falk that her father had returned the gun that very day.

Falk was sure Willie was afraid of the gun, but he knew she was a loyal friend who wanted to protect him against Quintero, who she likely recognized as her attacker.

Falk followed Quintero's stare at the girl while he weighed his options with the instincts of a fox. He probably saw what Falk noticed: a sudden, delicate dilation of the girl's pupils that might be a sign of indecision sparked by fear. Quintero lunged.

And met a bullet.

He arched backward. His beret flew into the air, and a dark red furrow parted skin and hairs above his left temple. But not for a moment did he lose his vise-like grip on the knife.

Immediately righting himself, he leapt forward, smashing a massive forearm across the side of the girl's head. The Beretta hurtled into the air and clattered to the floor at the agent's feet.

Falk caught his second wind and scooped up the gun just as

the Latino bolted towards the door and grabbed the briefcase.

"Hold it, amigo!" Falk shouted. His head was clear again. He gestured toward the chart table. "No more games. Put the knife and the case on the table, now." He watched the slick bastard affect an ingratiating posture.

"*Si, senor*," he said. With his forearm, he swiped at a thin line of blood that veined down his face, but made no move to comply.

A thunderbolt slammed the ship with such force it seemed to Falk that the rivets in her hull would pop. The lights flickered. Rain blurred every window and thrummed on the roof of the bridge. Willie, thrust to the floor by the force of her attacker's blow moments earlier, sat, dazed and gasping for the breath that had been knocked from her. Now she roused herself and rushed to Falk's side.

Falk again gestured to the man, raising his voice above the dissonance of another thunderclap.

"You have to the count of three to put the knife and the case on the table."

"*Si, si.*"

Slowly the man moved to the chart table and placed his blade on the wooden surface.

"The briefcase," Falk demanded.

But what Falk saw in the man's eyes was the realization of an advantage, and slowly, almost imperceptibly, the Latin slid the case up to an angle covering his chest, his neck, his chin and the lower part of his nose.

A flush of rage overtook Falk. He had underestimated his

adversary. Frozen in indecision, he felt Willie's eyes turn to him.

"Hul-lo," she said. "What's happening?" When Falk still did not move, he felt her pull at his pants leg. "Joe," she insisted, "shoot him like they do in the movies."

The man reached out, beckoning again toward Falk with his indecent fingers.

"We have one more hand to play, *senor.* The weapon, please."

"No!" Willie shouted, and stamped her feet. She stared at Falk. "Joe. The guy will kill us! Why don't you...?" her voice trailed off, as if she were finally aware of something of greater consequence in the moment. She released Falk's pants leg and moved slightly behind him.

The bastard knew Falk would not take the chance of hitting the briefcase being placed directly in the path of a bullet.

"Look, pal," Falk tried, "Put the case down or I'll shoot your balls off."

Quintero gave a sneering smile, sure that a gringo could never do such a thing.

Willie's voice was small again. "It's a bomb, isn't it?"

Falk sighed and pulled the trigger. Quintero's face tightened in disbelief as the 9 mm slug ripped into his scrotum, thinking in a silent scream, *An Americano would never do such a thing!*

As the briefcase slipped down his body, Falk fired a second shot and Quintero took it between the eyes, removing any doubt what this Americano would do.

# Chapter 54

Koski's sweaty, purple-red face rose from the dark space in the compartment beneath the chart table. She pushed farther up, her knees clearing the floor of the cupboard.

"What happened? Joe, you're hurt."

Despite the loss of blood, of which he was acutely aware, Falk sounded the depth of his own strength. "I'm okay, Koski. Look at you!"

"Joe shot the bad guy, Susan! He was going to kill us!" Willie ran to her side. "Where did you come from?"

Koski held the girl tight for a moment. "From way down in the ship."

Without warning, with no attendant sound but the wind and rain that lashed around him as he burst through the doorway from the exterior gangway and into the bridge, Simon Drummond halted at the chart room door, unsure of what he was seeing.

Drummond had spent the last few hours frantically trying to locate Bonecutter's bombs with help from his photocopied schematic. He'd found three of the sticky devices and removed the remote controlled detonators, but there were still seven and time was running out. He'd decided to make one last-ditch effort, hoping that some forgotten corner of the bridge would yield results.

Then, suddenly, the photograph he had taken from Marshak's "Pete Powers' envelope" came into focus in his mind. Drummond had studied the old picture again. He concluded that the man behind Angus Bonecutter in the chart room was not, as Drummond originally surmised, disappearing into the room's focal point, but into the partially constructed floor. He was about to descend into an interior passageway, possibly leading to the lower decks. This he saw as his last hope of finding the briefcase, somewhere between the bridge and the decks below.

Now, however, none of that seemed to matter. The Girl Scout that Beard had mentioned sat on a low bench at the back of the room, next to the female agent Drummond recognized from the blow-up in Beard's office.

The other agent, he knew from a similar photo, was Joseph Falk, known to British Intelligence as the man who cracked the case of the murdered lawyers. He had literally saved the U.S. from total domestic and economic disaster.

In the present instance, however, Falk looked considerably worse for the wear and his clothes were stained with blood. He stood next to the body of a man stretched out on the floor whom Drummond knew to be a terrorist.

Everyone in the room froze in silence at Drummond's unexpected appearance. Then Falk reached down and wrenched the briefcase from Quintero's fingers.

Falk turned to Koski, who seemed numb and was

mechanically hugging the child, shielding her eyes from the sight of close-up death. Renewing his grip on the briefcase, Falk shot a glance at the chart room clock: seven-forty-five. If Bonecutter had not been apprehended, they had exactly fifteen minutes to get off the ship before all hell broke loose.

He gently but urgently touched his partner's shoulder. "Koski...Bonecutter?" She lowered her eyes and silently shook her head. He turned to Drummond with the same question in his eyes, but Drummond opened his arms in a futile gesture and shrugged.

"Come on," Falk said. "We've got to get out of here." He nudged Koski's elbow, and she rose from the bench, one arm still around Willie, whose face was partially buried against Koski's sweater.

Falk thought that they, himself included, must look as if they had just returned from a war zone. Although unhurt, Drummond was soaked from rain and disheveled from hours of rummaging into musty corners of the ship.

The Englishman now wore a shell-shocked expression from the scene he'd walked into. The body of a professional murderer who, moments before, was alive and ready to kill them, lay before him. Willie, too, was obviously mentally and physically in tatters. A contusion swelled above her right eye from the force of Quintero's earlier blow.

As Koski passed in front of him, Falk wanted to take her in his arms and hug her and, somehow, erase the pain of this long day.

Her clothes were stained with dirt and dust. Her glorious

blonde hair wildly crisscrossed her head and clung with perspiration to her forehead. The odors of urine and liquor hovered around her, replacing, for a time, the scent of Savon Doux Place des Lices Pivoine.

Falk knew how much she must have struggled to overcome her claustrophobia. She might have lost control and tumbled to her death, but she didn't. They were a team, links in a never-ending chain of unsung men and women who affected world events in a positive way. How much he loved her at this very moment.

"Hurry!" Drummond said, awakening from his shock.

Falk pushed the two females into the wheelhouse, still ignoring the knife wound that continued to dampen his side.

Lightning zigzagged into the bridge, a sharp, prolonged series of electrical flashes bolting across the sky. Before the outburst ended, all but a few scattered lights on the ship sizzled out, and most of the vessel was plunged into darkness. A nearby transformer had been knocked out, Falk guessed, as rolls of ear-splitting thunder followed its eternal partner across the sky.

Then Falk heard a familiar, nasal voice in his ear-bud."Falk, Beard here. Do you have the compound?"

"Affirmative. And I have Koski, the Englishman, and the girl with me. The Latin is dead."

"And Bonecutter?"

"We don't know where he is, but he's got the bombs on him. Seven as far as we know. Drummond found three and disarmed them."

"Okay. Get your party off the ship immediately," Beard

ordered. Then, in the next breath, "'On him' you say? Are they still armed?"

"We believe he defused them, but if one fuse, or even portion of one, is left in one of those babies..."

Beard cut in. "Well, in any case, he's no longer your responsibility. Get off the ship! Now!"

The reception was clear, no static. As Falk surmised earlier, static and dead spots in parts of the ship were due to steel and iron construction. On deck and in the bridge area the Bluetooth system posed no problem.

He didn't like being told to leave without having found Bonecutter. Yes, the man was dangerous, but the poor bastard was sick and might possibly still blow up the ship. Then a wave of dizziness washed over him and he shoved the briefcase into Drummond's arms.

"Go!" he hollered.

They faced a cold blast of wind and rain as they left the wheelhouse and trooped down the gangway.

"Follow the gangplank escalator," he shouted to Drummond, who led.

# Chapter 55

Wind roared through every open portion of the ship, and rain battered every surface, producing an almost musical steel drum sound as water hurtled itself against metal. Except for shore lights trained on her port side, the ship was now in darkness.

While the others raced on ahead, Falk halted at the bottom of the gangway, a lightning flash causing him to look to his right, where a section of the bow was still illuminated. There he saw movement on the foreword mainmast.

Squinting into the storm, he looked up. His breath caught when he saw Jack Bonecutter in the crow's nest high above the deck, his body strobed by lightning, winking like a full moon intermittently obscured by clouds.

"Shit!" Falk whispered.

"It figures," Drummond hissed when the three reached the escalator, and he saw that Falk was not with them. They huddled beneath a huge, blue canopy that covered the gangplank at the top of the unmoving stairs.

"That agent's more than an idiot. Probably found Bonecutter," Drummond said. "It seems to be his nature to be the hero."

Koski's benumbed state following her ascent in the shaft and the horror of the chart room having passed, she was once again Special Agent Koski again.

"Here." She handed Drummond the chemical wrap she had kept in her pocket.

"Take this and Willie and get down to the dock," Koski shouted. "That man's my partner, and I'm going back for him."

Drummond saw a ring of police and army personnel gathering on the dock below. The Haz-Mat unit stood by to deal with the myriad hazardous materials they might encounter.

Drummond recalled the PM's voice from earlier today, telling him not to let the amalgam out of his sight if and when he found it. "Above all else," the PM had told him on the phone, "we have to get our hands on that briefcase, Drummond."

Drummond understood what "above all else" meant. Get off the ship with the highly desired briefcase in possession. He had been fully prepared for that and had came through the ordeal comparatively unscathed, but without the briefcase. Now, here was the briefcase, being offered to him, and his chance for undying glory.

As Koski turned and charged back toward the bow of the ship, Drummond unceremoniously whipped the chemical wrap around the briefcase, tucked it under one arm as if it were an old newspaper, swept Willie into his arms, and started down the large, grooved, metal stairs.

"We've done our good deed for today," he whispered, unsure if Willie heard.

# Chapter 56

For Bonecutter, high above the decks, this was the resolution of his experience as a three-year-old, and the reclaiming of his life. It was the completion of a scene, which, too long, had survived behind his eyelids, never wholly having been acted out.

"Whee," he screeched above the sound of wind and thunder. "Whee, little Jack."

Every detail of that long-ago trauma flooded into his mind, as if he had stored up the abuse, waiting for this moment to fully unleash it.

As the wind hurled rain at him, he leaned out over the rim of the crow's nest and slipped the souvenir bag from his shoulder, offering it to the storm.

"Whee. Whe-e-e."

The image of his grandfather took on flesh and impulse. Bonecutter was spirit, playing out the terror again and again. But it was too late for exorcism. There was nothing left but revenge, before his world went totally and violently insane.

# Chapter 57

Falk passed the bridge gangway and stumbled across the bow deck. The klieg lights from the dock hardly penetrated the heavy, wind-driven rain. He could see the fore-rigging, jerking and clanking violently this way and that.

When he got to the rope ladder Bonecutter had used to climb to the crow's nest, which Falk thought to use to get to the man, it broke loose at its base due to the pummeling of the wind. It flapped dangerously about in the air, whacking against the mainmast, twisting and turning like a furious snake finally freed from the restraints that bound it.

Frantically, Falk sought another way to save the deranged man. He took a step forward and stopped, feeling something beneath his shoe. Looking down, in the profound darkness he couldn't tell for certain, but it looked like a pager. He bent down and picked it up. A remote control.

Bonecutter's remote.

It must have fallen. That meant Bonecutter couldn't detonate the bombs. A wave of relief washed over Falk. Yet, why did a foreboding sense of time escaping, hissing away like air from a pricked balloon, still press against his heart?

He looked up again, the rain pelting his upturned face, and heard Bonecutter screeching, saw him leaning far out over the rim of the bucket and laughing a lunatic laugh that could be heard above the storm.

It seemed that, any second, he would topple from his precarious perch as he swung a plastic bag in his outstretched arms toward the lightning that, again, lit the sky.

The bag. Falk thought. The plastic bag full of bombs.

Grim foreboding turned to concern and then outright fear. Beard had said that Bonecutter defused the bombs, but if even one fuse remained, even a portion of one, anything could still set them off even without the detonator.

There was a sudden, deafening silence. Then a splintering crack, as if the sky split above them. Falk whirled and saw Koski rushing toward him, ready to help, unaware of what Falk would know in nightmares for the rest of his life.

In that chilling moment of supernatural clarity, Falk lunged headlong through the air, tackling Koski and propelling them both as far as he could from the death he saw coming, while pinning them to the deck behind the thick metal gangway of the bridge.

Thunder and lightning collided in the sky overhead. The sound, like a million crashing thunderbolts, screamed through the air. A long flash of lightning hit the crow's nest, snaking its sizzling tendrils into the bag Bonecutter was holding out and rocketed life into the one partially armed explosive.

In one instant, Bonecutter there, in the next he was a sparkler, a core of white-hot energy of electricity gone mad, spiking incandescent flares into the ebony sky.

The next moment, he and the nest that had nurtured his madness were blown apart, the detonation hurtling rigging, scraps of metal, and shards of human debris in every possible direction.

Before he forced his eyes to shut, Falk saw bulbs of flame, like comets, rip into the bow, splintering the heavy wooden deck planks into shreds. Wet wood went furiously aflame. Chunks of steel, timber, rope and glass torpedoed everywhere, exploding windows and ripping holes in the wood about them.

# Chapter 58

Falk swam against the waves of sleep that washed over him threatening to sent him back to a hideous dream of death. Drummond appeared. He ran, racing to get off the ship but couldn't get off soon enough. The vessel exploded around him; the briefcase he carried burst into a million malignant molecules and diseased cells spewed and wriggled in the scorching, burning, debris-filled air. The malevolent pieces buried themselves like leeches in his flesh.

Falk thought he screamed.

Then he slept again, until, at last, knew he was dreaming, as the tide he swam against became a voice.

"Joe? Joe?"

His mouth was sour. He gulped saliva that tasted of rust and kept escaping from lips that felt weighed down. Slowly he opened his eyes.

"You're going to be okay, Joe." It was Koski. She was safe. But her words quivered with tears. "You've got bruises, and lacerations, and you've lost a lot of blood from the knife wound, but you're going to be all right."

He tried to raise his head and look around, but even the slight movement of his eyes made his head hurt. After a few seconds it became clear he was on a gurney, no doubt on his way to an ambulance. His head was bandaged; a mask hissed over his nose and mouth mouth, and the IVs in his arms were attached to bags of fluids held high in the air by a paramedic who walked briskly along his right side.

"Koski," Falk rasped. "You okay?"

She was walking on the other side of the rolling stretcher, which was propelled by another paramedic at Falk's feet. Her warm hand held his, and she bent down toward him as he was jostled along.

"I'm fine," she whispered. "Thanks to you. You saved my life."

"Good," he barely got out. "And Willy?"

"In the ambulance that just left. Her parents are with her. She was banged up some, and has a slight concussion, but she'll be fine. Her Girl Scout troop is already calling her a hero."

She didn't wait for his next three questions.

"The briefcase is intact, safely contained in the chemical wrap and on its way to a secret location. No doubt it will be the subject of years of discussions between the British and American governments and a source of wild speculation on the part of the press."

So it was over, Falk thought. Hopefully, the world would never have to know the weapon's true sinister potential; or that two so-called peace-loving nations had commissioned its creation. He sighed, letting go of the sense of obligation that lifted from his shoulders.

He thought of the scientist in Panama, and what anguish he must have suffered during his years of exile. Maybe the three traditional words invoked at funerals and etched into countless headstones would, in the old man's case, finally be prophetic.

Koski murmured some encouraging remarks, but Falk momentarily lost her words. His heart was light and his senses seemed to be soaring. Another huge sigh caused his body to seem to float in air.

Finally, "Drummond?" Falk asked.

"Fit as a fiddle, thanks to you."

"Where is he?"

"In Beard's office, being debriefed. I heard him acting Mr. Humble in there, constantly praising you. But the press is making such a fuss over him. Looks like he is going to be an international hero."

Falk squeezed her hand. "So Willie and Drummond are heroes, are they? What does that make you, Koski?"

At first she registered surprise at the question, then a small smile. "I'm enough to be me."

Falk thought that this was probably the most inappropriate time for the words he was about to say, but a fine, warm certainty made him utter them. "Know what I'm going to be?"

"What?"

"A husband. If you'll have me."

Koski bolted straight up and stopped as the gurney continued on and was wheeled to the open doors of the ambulance. She watched in surprise as its wheels folded under and it was pushed into the back of the vehicle. Then she caught up, and they let her hustle in beside him.

She huddled close to his face.

"I guess I need to go to the hospital, too," she whispered with dead seriousness. "To be checked out. I think I'm hearing things that couldn't possibly have been said."

An exquisite tiredness came over Falk, and he slipped back into a much needed sleep.

# Epilogue

As the ambulance passed the mobile command post, Marshak was in his small office, packing up his paperwork. He had his wife on the speakerphone.

She said, "Thank God you're safe, Bukka."

"Of course I'm safe, woman."

"The bomber, he's dead?"

"Yes."

During the long hours that constituted this tragic day, Marshak had given more thought to the man and his motives. "You know," he told his wife, "I've been thinking that maybe the guy didn't really care so much about destroying this ship as he seemed to let on."

He looked around the room as if checking to be sure no one else heard him make what he thought was a pseudo-psychological concession.

"Maybe, for some weird reason that we'll never know, that maybe even Bonecutter didn't know, he subconsciously hated the ship. And maybe he had a damned good reason to want to wreck her."

"Maybe," his wife acknowledged, uncomprehending. "Has

General Beard gone?"

"Colonel Beard?" Marshak corrected. "No, not yet; he's about to talk to the reporters. I understand that 'we', meaning the United States Army, are taking full credit for the success of this operation."

"Success? But we all watched on television most of the bridge and bow of the ship blown away."

"Well, she didn't sink. And since the damage was confined to the upper decks, she's repairable. But the main thing is, only two lives were lost." He looked around the room again. "And some secret hazardous material, that would have poisoned the entire planet if we hadn't found it, is safely on its way to an undisclosed underground lab. Of course, that's between us."

He paused to drag on a cigarette before concluding, "I knew, first thing when I got up this morning, this day was going to be a doozy."

# About the Author

Multi-award winning author A. G. Hayes studied television writing at UCLA and has published short fiction, including "Cover up," "Not a Penny Pincher," "Home," "Payment in Full," "Small Wonder," "Guided Through a Mine Field" and other scripts to CBS TV and other television productions. He lives in Northern California, and spends his time writing and traveling to nearly every part of the world. He has used personal experiences gained during service with the British intelligence in Eastern Europe and the Middle East to enrich the characters of his protagonist teams. Savant publications include WHO'S KILLING ALL THE LAWYERS? (2011), THE JUDAS LIST (2012), and IMMINENT DANGER (2013).

If you enjoyed *The Chemical Factor* consider the first book in the Falk and Koski adventure series, the Kindle genre bestseller, *Who's Killing All the Lawyers?* by A. G. Hayes:

*Lawyers are being murdered by laser-driven arrows. The FBI believes that someone is training a Native American militia to take over the economic system in the U.S. Joe Falk and Susan Koski are assigned to find the hired killer and The Fox, the real force behind the killings.*

…the second book in the Falk and Koski adventure series, *The Judas List* by A. G. Hayes:

*Between the end of World War II and the winter of 1975, a 700-year-old prayer book, a key and a faded blueprint came to light in Vienna, and began a 25-year search for Nazi Herman Goering's treasure. In modern day Vienna, American agents Koski and Falk must go undercover to locate the treasure and the Judas List—a compendium of individuals and organizations that financed WWII, and, in it's aftermath, now intended to manipulate world finances to bring about the Fourth Reich. But the Americans aren't the only ones looking for the list and the treasure. So are ex-Nazi, the Bosnians, Russians and, most recently, Muslim militants.*

…and the third book in the Koski and Falk adventure series, *Imminent Danger* by A. G. Hayes:

*Jamul, an adored American pop singer, dreams of a grand show of Islamic Jihad power, intending to use a biological weapon to eradicate religious leaders at an Easter service at the Hollywood Bowl. In response, Cerberus agents Joe Falk and Susan Koski must seek help from unlikely sources-gang bangers, scientists and the public-to stop the next brutal terrorist attack on American soil.*

Coming Soon: The fifth book in the Koski and Falk adventure series, *Quantum Death*:

Koski and Falk come up against what very well may prove to be their most complex and dangerous case yet: The Quantum Death Machine. For the first time, Koski and Falk must separate during a mission. Each faces mortal peril, while, at the same time, their smoldering relationship continues to heat up.

If you enjoyed *The Chemical Factor,* consider these other fine books from
Savant Books and Publications:

*Essay, Essay, Essay* by Yasuo Kobachi
*Aloha from Coffee Island* by Walter Miyanari
*Footprints, Smiles and Little White Lies* by Daniel S. Janik
*The Illustrated Middle Earth* by Daniel S. Janik
*Last and Final Harvest* by Daniel S. Janik
*A Whale's Tale* by Daniel S. Janik
*Tropic of California* by R. Page Kaufman
*Tropic of California* (the companion music CD) by R. Page Kaufman
*The Village Curtain* by Tony Tame
*Dare to Love in Oz* by William Maltese
*The Interzone* by Tatsuyuki Kobayashi
*Today I Am a Man* by Larry Rodness
*The Bahrain Conspiracy* by Bentley Gates
*Called Home* by Gloria Schumann
*Kanaka Blues* by Mike Farris
*First Breath* edited by Z. M. Oliver
*Poor Rich* by Jean Blasiar
*The Jumper Chronicles* by W. C. Peever
*William Maltese's Flicker* by William Maltese
*My Unborn Child* by Orest Stocco
*Last Song of the Whales* by Four Arrows
*Perilous Panacea* by Ronald Klueh
*Falling but Fulfilled* by Zachary M. Oliver
*Mythical Voyage* by Robin Ymer
*Hello, Norma Jean* by Sue Dolleris
*Richer* by Jean Blasiar
*Manifest Intent* by Mike Farris
*Charlie No Face* by David B. Seaburn
*Number One Bestseller* by Brian Morley
*My Two Wives and Three Husbands* by S. Stanley Gordon
*In Dire Straits* by Jim Currie
*Wretched Land* by Mila Komarnisky
*Chan Kim* by Ilan Herman
*Who's Killing All the Lawyers?* by A. G. Hayes
*Ammon's Horn* by G. Amati
*Wavelengths* edited by Zachary M. Oliver
*Almost Paradise* by Laurie Hanan
*Communion* by Jean Blasiar and Jonathan Marcantoni
*The Oil Man* by Leon Puissegur
*Random Views of Asia from the Mid-Pacific* by William E. Sharp
*The Isla Vista Crucible* by Reilly Ridgell
*Blood Money* by Scott Mastro
*In the Himalayan Nights* by Anoop Chandola
*On My Behalf* by Helen Doan

*Traveler's Rest* by Jonathan Marcantoni
*Keys in the River* by Tendai Mwanaka
*Chimney Bluffs* by David B. Seaburn
*The Loons* by Sue Dolleris
*Light Surfer* by David Allan Williams
*The Judas List* by A. G. Hayes
*Path of the Templar—Book 2 of The Jumper Chronicles* by W. C. Peever
*The Desperate Cycle* by Tony Tame
*Shutterbug* by Buz Sawyer
*Blessed are the Peacekeepers* by Tom Donnelly and Mike Munger
*The Bellwether Messages* edited by D. S. Janik
*The Turtle Dances* by Daniel S. Janik
*The Lazarus Conspiracies* by Richard Rose
*Purple Haze* by George B. Hudson
*Imminent Danger* by A. G. Hayes
*Lullaby Moon* (CD) by Malia Elliott of Leon & Malia
*Volutions* edited by Suzanne Langford
*In the Eyes of the Son* by Hans Brinckmann
*The Hanging of Dr. Hanson* by Bentley Gates
*Flight of Destiny* by Francis Powell
*Elaine of Corbenic* by Tima Z. Newman
*Ballerina Birdies* by Marina Yamamoto
*More More Time* by David B. Seabird
*Crazy Like Me* by Erin Lee
*Cleopatra Unconquered* by Helen R. Davis
*Valedictory* by Daniel Scott

Coming Soon:
*All Things Await* by Seth Clabough
*Big Heaven* by Charlotte Hebert
*Captain Riddle's Treasure* by GV Rama Rao
*Tsunami Libido* by Cate Burns
*Quantum Death* by A. G. Hayes
*The Adventures of Purple Head, Buddha Monkey and Sticky Feet* by Erik Bracht

http://www.savantbooksandpublications.com